THE RAIDERS OF DEATH

"You were in Missouri, and you killed an innocent woman and her two children, and now you will die for your crime." Before Riley could move, Rontrell had lifted his pistol and slammed a .44 lead slug into Riley's right arm. The bone shattered and blood gushed out, making a scarlet streak on the gray earth.

"Bastard!" Riley screamed. "Fight me like a man! Let me loose and give me a chance!"

"You get no more chance than you gave that woman three years ago, Riley. You want to confess before you die?"

Riley shook his head. "I was never *in* Missouri."

Mary looked up. "But you told me about how during the war you rode in Missouri, and that you were looking for food and supplies, and that you did see some action."

"I was in Tennessee, Mary. Never in Missouri!"

Rontrell laughed and shot Riley in the stomach.

Riley sagged against the ropes that held him. Pain shattered his face; he moaned, his breath coming in gasps.

"Gut shot; you could live an hour, Riley. The pain is terrible. You want to confess now?"

The first book in a rip-roaring, new western series

SPUR #1:

HIGH PLAINS
TEMPTRESS

Dirk Fletcher

LEISURE BOOKS ∞ NEW YORK CITY

A LEISURE BOOK

Published by

Nordon Publications, Inc.
Two Park Avenue
New York, N.Y. 10016

ONE

FARGO, KANSAS, SEPTEMBER 1867

They rode out of the west, six men with hard eyes, red and blue handkerchief masks over their faces, dressed in well-worn, nondescript range and town clothes.

They came to kill.

The first spears of dawn were shattering the eastern horizon in the monotonously flat Kansas plains. Far to the right the Flint Hills were the first to pick up the actual light of the new day.

Leading the band was a man called Rontrell. In the semidarkness he motioned to the men, who now could see the dim outlines of the ranch buildings ahead. They knew what to do. He sent two men around to the left to come up behind the small bunkhouse. There could be one, maybe two, hands sleeping there. The raiders would ground–tie their horses a quarter of a mile from the shack and run up to the target silently.

The head man sent two more riders to the left. They would check the small barn, come in the rear and aim rifles out the door, covering the house. The men rode off without a word, heeding their training and instructions. As long as everyone did exactly what he was told the raid would be successful.

Rontrell took the last man with him. They rode toward the four-room ranch house made of shiplap, which was now spouting wood-fire smoke from a good-sized blaze. They would ride up to the front door, like any trail rider hunting directions.

The raiders knew their jobs and understood the purpose of this mission. On the long ride from town, Rontrell had briefed them.

"Tonight we're going to execute a man," he had said. "This man is a killer at least three times over. He's scum; he doesn't deserve to live. He murdered a woman and her two small children without a thought. He deserves to die. We're going after him, but if his wife or any of the hands get in the way we'll do what we have to to guarantee success."

He had checked the eyes above the men's masks. Rontrell insisted on the masks, since not every man in the group knew every other one, and it was best at this point to keep the action teams unaware of all the identities. The eyes above the masks were hard, slightly angry, ready to do whatever he told them, ready to believe that what he said was the gospel truth.

"A murderer like Clyde Riley deserves whatever he gets. Riley is a swine, a coldblooded murderer. Maybe some of you know him. We have to put aside personal feelings; we have a job to do, a mission, and

6

we will complete it."

After that he got them moving again so they wouldn't think too much about it. Now as the outline of the house came into view he felt the old excitement stir within him, as in the days when he had been always in the saddle, when he had had a band of followers who knew their duty to God and country and followed him on any attack, anywhere. His heartbeat jumped as his chest tightened in anticipation.

Rontrell expected Riley to come out of the house with a weapon, but he wouldn't be suspicious. He thought he was free and clear. The rifles in the barn would take care of any problem of Riley's arming himself.

The dawn was upon them as they swung around the small gate and rode up to the house. A short hitching rail near the back porch was their goal. Before they got there a man stepped off the back porch. It was Clyde Riley, and he cradled a double-barreled shotgun over his left forearm, his finger on the trigger.

"That's far enough, strangers. Why the hell are you wearing those masks?" Riley brought up the shotgun and the two horsemen stopped. "I don't know who the hell you are, but drop them masks, right now."

Rontrell distorted his voice, as he always did on a raid, so it couldn't be recognized. "No, Riley. Two rifles have a bead on you from your barn door. Drop the shotgun or you and your wife are dead."

Riley looked toward the barn. It was beyond the range of the scatter gun. He saw the rifle barrels slanting from the black hole of the door. With a sigh he lowered the shotgun.

"Lay it on the ground, Riley."

Riley did and then took a few steps toward the riders.

"Hey, don't I know you, mister? You with them Rontrell Raiders?" He frowned, and sweat popped out on his forehead. "What you guys want?"

"Just want to ask you a few questions," Rontrell said. He swung down from the horse and tied it to the hitching rail. The rider beside him copied his motions. They were careful not to get between Riley and the two rifles in the barn.

"Your wife inside, Riley?"

He nodded.

"Tell her not to do anything stupid like getting a gun, and tell her to come out here now."

"Why?"

"Because I said so, and we have the guns," Rontrell said in his growling rumble.

Riley called to his wife, who came out wiping her hands on an apron. Her face was frightened, worried. She went to her husband and stood beside him.

Rontrell touched his hand to his black wide-brimmed hat. "Ma'am, I wanted you to know about your husband. Before he came to Kansas his name was Lawrence Bedford."

Riley stared at Rontrell. "Why the hell you calling me that? My name's always been Riley."

"I know a lot about you, Bedford. I know that three years ago you were riding in Missouri with a band of raiders, and you burned a farm near the little town of Mapleton. The farmer was killed in the first exchange of gunfire. Then you brought out his wife and a girl of six and a boy of eight and brutally murdered all three of them, before you burned the buildings, took the cattle and supplies, and rode off."

"That's a lie!" Riley shouted.

Rontrell remained calm. "Every killer says the same thing," he said. "There were witnesses, some of your own men. You were put on report but before anything could be done the war was over. Now the authorities are taking action on that report."

I was never *in* Missouri!" Riley yelled, his voice going high, his eyes wild.

"We know you were." Rontrell turned to his masked companion. "Tie Riley to the porch post." Two more men ran up from the bunkhouse. They said that no one was there, and they helped tie Riley to the post.

Rontrell looked up in time to see Riley's wife storming at him, her hands up, fingernails clawing at his face. One hand got past his defending arm and nearly reached his cheek. Rontrell slapped her, reached for her. His hand caught the front of her dress and, as she pulled away, the bodice of the garment ripped loose and fell to her waist, revealing only a thin cotton chemise covering her breasts. She fell to her knees, wailing and covering herself with her arms.

"You bastard!" Riley screamed. "Leave Mary alone. Do you always fight with women? Let me loose and I'll take care of you!"

Rontrell shook his head. "You were in Missouri,

and you killed an innocent woman and her two children, and now you will die for your crime." Before Riley could move, Rontrell lifted his pistol and slammed a .44 lead slug into Riley's right arm. The bone shattered and blood gushed out, making a scarlet streak on the gray earth.

"Bastard!" Riley screamed. "Fight me like a man! Let me loose and give me a chance!"

"You get no more chance than you gave that woman three years ago, Riley. You want to confess before you die?"

Riley shook his head. "I was never in Missouri."

Mary looked up. "But you told me about how during the war you rode in Missouri, and that you were looking for food and supplies, and that you did see some action."

"I was in Tennessee, Mary. Never in Missouri!"

Rontrell laughed and shot Riley in the stomach.

Riley sagged against the ropes that held him. Pain shattered his face; he moaned, his breath coming in gasps.

"Gut shot; you could live an hour, Riley. The pain is terrible. You want to confess now?"

Riley looked at him, eyes glinting with hellish pain and anger. He spat at his tormentor, but the wetness missed Rontrell.

"You'll burn in hell for this, whoever you are," Riley said. The rancher looked at his executioner again. "Yeah, now I know you. Seen you in town lots of times. Voice fooled me." Riley coughed and spit blood. "My God, you've killed me!" He looked at Mary. "Mary," he called weakly. "This damn masked man is that guy who—"

10

Rontrell's Colt spoke twice and both slugs rammed through Riley's thin blue shirt and drilled on through his heart. He never finished the sentence.

Mary Riley put both hands over her face when the gun fired again. Then she looked quickly, saw her husband fall forward against the ropes. She sat in the dust, wailing in sudden realization that he was dead.

Rontrell mounted and holstered his Colt. He motioned for the two men from the barn to return to their horses. Rontrell signaled the two men from the bunkhouse back to their mounts a quarter of a mile away.

The raiders' leader looked down at the new widow. "Mrs. Riley, you're a fine-looking woman. You won't have any trouble finding a new husband. Riley was a killer; you're better off without him." He pulled the mount's head around and galloped off down the lane toward the road that led back to town. One more down, one more debt paid, and one more advance made in the march toward his eventual goal. A grim feeling of satisfaction warmed him as he jogged along toward the other men half a mile ahead.

An hour later they split up, all six taking different routes into town from various compass points and at different times. There would be no suspicion. They unmasked only after they split up.

Rontrell lowered his mask into a rolled kerchief around his neck and rode into Fargo from the side nearest his house so he wouldn't have to go through the main part of town. He saw no one but the mayor's wife, who was half a block down the street and didn't notice him. Rontrell rode to his small stable behind his big house on Elm Street.

One more murderer had met his maker. Another victory, another moment of justice. He put away his horse, brushed her down, then put in a can of oats for the mare and walked up the steps to the back door of his house.

TWO

Spur McCoy woke with a start; a chilly wind was blowing across his naked torso. He looked at the curtains billowing in the window and shook his head. It had cooled off considerably during the night —but then this was Denver, Colorado Territory.

He wondered for a moment where he was, then remembered the girl. This was her room. He turned and looked at her, snoring softly, her head cradled in her hands as she slept peacefully on her side.

What was her name? Spur couldn't remember. Not that it mattered; he wouldn't be seeing her again. She was tame in bed, almost virginal. She hadn't seemed to enjoy the sex. Spur couldn't remember a woman he'd had less pleasure with. Eventually he'd rolled over and dropped off to sleep.

The girl hadn't said a word the whole time, but she had looked as unhappy as he. At least he'd gotten a good night's sleep.

Spur lay back in the small bed, staring out the window as dawn colored the sky. Sunrise would

13

come and be gone in minutes; he might as well attempt to slip out of the girl's room without waking her, to avoid the moment of mutual embarrassment when they looked into one another's eyes. This time, Spur thought, the morning after made the night before far from worth the effort.

He swung his feet out from the sheet and quilts, rested them on the cold wooden floor, and stood. In a full-length mirror across the room he caught a glimpse of himself, his muscled, naked body almost gray in the near darkness of the room. For a moment Spur stood before the mirror, checking his reflection; he was still in good shape.

Years of hard work and outdoor living had paid off. Spur had a body that most men were jealous of and most women desired. Not an inch of excess fat showed on his six-foot-two frame, while his arms, chest and legs rippled with muscles.

His sandy red hair was too long; he'd have to get it cut. Stubble poked out on his jaw and neck and around his muttonchop sideburns and full red moustache. In the growing light he briefly glanced at the rest of his face; at the planed, masculine look that women found attractive; the green eyes and hard chin.

He felt an ache in his right shoulder and rubbed the throbbing spot; he must have lain on it wrong. Spur moved from the mirror and across the room to his pants and pulled them on, then wrapped his torso in his blue flannel shirt. He tucked and buttoned, then bent to retrieve his boots and woolen socks.

As he gripped the boots and rose to his full height,

14

he felt the pressure of a muzzle against his spine. He dropped the boots, then turned and knocked the firearm to the floor before recognizing the laughing girl's face.

She picked up the Colt .44 and handed it to him.

"Don't do that again," Spur said, looking at her sternly. "Never play with guns—at least not around me." He sat on the bed, stuffed his feet into the woolen socks and reached for the boots.

"Where are you going?" she asked sleepily.

"Out. I need a shave and I want to see if I have to leave town." He removed the spurs from the boots.

"I could shave you," she suggested.

"No. I don't trust women with razors."

"It's the least I can do, after last night . . . ." The girl moved into the light now streaming through the bedroom window and Spur saw again what had attracted him to her. Blonde hair fell in tiny ringlets to her shoulders. She shook her head once and stared at him, her head at a cockeyed angle. Her eyes were light blue and flashing; the lips full and as red as cherry cider. She stood naked and he looked down at her heavy, full breasts, tiny waist and flaring hips.

Even in the harsh morning sunlight she was a beautiful young woman, Spur thought with misgivings. If only she were better in bed! He shook his head, picked up a boot and wrestled it on.

"No?" she said. "I feel awful about last night." She moved to sit beside him. "It's not your fault, it's Homer's. He's my late husband. He didn't want me to like sex, so I guess he taught me how to hate it. It's hard to get back to normal."

"Your late husband? How old are you?" Spur

15

asked, not believing she could have been married.

"Twenty-two," she said. "I'm sorry. What do you say we try it again? Take off those britches and take me to bed." She licked one finger and touched it to her breast.

Spur looked at her, then shook his head again. "Sorry. I have to go out and get some things done. Maybe later."

"Will you be in Denver long?" she asked, standing and stepping into a petticoat.

"Don't know for sure," Spur said, as he got his second boot on and fastened on the spurs.

"Well, keep me in mind. I'm really not anything like you saw me last night," she said, trying to smile but doing a poor job of it.

"It isn't your fault." Spur stood and holstered the Colt she'd played with, bent to peck her cheek, and walked to the door.

"See you," he said, and left.

He didn't mean to be cruel to the woman, but she'd been a disappointment. He'd been working his butt off finishing a case involving stolen gold. He hadn't had a woman for weeks and she'd let him down.

Spur sighed and he walked out of the hotel and into the morning air, which was tinged with the first hint of fall. Smoke rose from several stone chimneys, scenting the air, and the street was already full of people going about their business.

He headed down the muddy street toward the telegraph office. He should receive a new assignment from the general soon; he'd wired two days ago that he had finished the gold case in Denver, and General

16

Halleck usually had something for him to do.

It had been a short hop from a career as a Civil War army captain to being aide in Washington to Senator Arthur B. Walton, an old family friend, Spur thought as he mused about his present employment. In 1865 Spur was appointed a U.S. Secret Service agent. At first the Secret Service was concerned only with preventing currency counterfeiting, but since it was the sole federal law-enforcement agency, it began handling a wide range of problems.

Spur had served in the Secret Service office in Washington for six months, and was then transferred to head the base in St. Louis and to handle all the action west of the Mississippi. Spur wondered at the time why he'd been chosen out of the ten men considered, and was rather chagrined when he later found he was the only man who could ride a horse well.

Of course his boss, William Wood, told him the fact that he'd won the service marksmanship contest had weighed in his decision as well. Wood needed a man who could ride and shoot.

On his way to the telegraph office, Spur decided it was too early for a message to have come through, so he detoured and went to his hotel. In his room he sat on the bed and broke down, then oiled, his Winchester repeating rifle, the 1866 model, and his Colt .44. After that, feeling grimy, he went to the dresser, poured water into the basin, and gave himself a whore's bath, scrubbing his body with a rough cotton cloth from head to toe.

Refreshed, Spur dried, climbed back into his

clothes, and decided he was hungry. Maybe he could catch a bite of breakfast.

He holstered his Colt, locked his door, and went downstairs, but the table had been cleared; he should have noticed that breakfast was over when he came in by the kitchen. Cursing himself, Spur headed outside and went to the barber shop.

A young barber stood sharpening a razor on a strop. "Hiya," he said courteously as Spur walked in.

"Same to you," Spur said, smelling the lime and bay cologne that permeated the shop. He sat in the solitary chair and put his feet up. "How about a shave and a haircut?"

"Shore," the man said. "You're my first man today. The towels are still nice and hot." With that he turned his back, then came toward Spur with a steaming gray cloth. He slapped it down on Spur's face and whistled while he lathered some soap in a shaving mug.

After a moment the barber removed the cloth, lathered Spur, then started scraping his cheeks, humming a tuneless song, from which he periodically broke to make small talk.

The barber wiped Spur's face and, without asking, slapped a handful of the sickly smelling bay rum on his cheeks. The haircut took longer with the hand clippers and snapping scissors, and Spur was glad when it was over.

He thanked the barber, handed him two bits and walked outside. Spur went to the telegraph office, and the harried man motioned for him to sit down; he was busily scratching out letters on a fat pad of

18

paper. When he was through and the chattering sound of the machine had ceased, Spur rose and asked if any messages had come in for Spur McCoy. The man checked, grabbed a sheet of paper and handed it to him.

"Here," he said. "That's all."

"Thanks." Spur walked out of the office and took the message into the sunlight. There he read his next assignment.

"Spur McCoy, Denver: Proceed to Fargo, Kansas. Trouble with freebooting raiders who have killed and burned. Organized, terrorizing the town. Go in, investigate the group, use army assistance if required, capture or destroy the leaders, nullify the group's effectiveness, and report back when job is completed.
                    J. Jones,
                    Law Assistance League"

Spur stared at the paper. Halleck was using his usual caution, standard for Secret Service activities. Spur had received more than a dozen wires from "J. Jones," and countless others bearing different names, all from General Halleck. Most also used "Law Assistance League" or some other nondescript name, which would be meaningless to prying eyes.

Freebooters? He looked at the message again. He hadn't heard of them since the War. Freebooters were authorized raiders from both the South and the North who struck into enemy territory, burned and looted, then returned to their own lines with booty

19

and supplies to help their own cause.

Now it seemed someone had dusted off the idea and was using similar-type raiders to wage some sort of personal war against Fargo, Kansas. Spur had heard of the town before; it was one of the division points of the railroad, and he'd even been there last year during a stop on the train.

He shrugged, folded the wire and stuffed it into his pocket. At least it was a different assignment. Fargo. The place was 350 miles away, so he'd take the train. One came through at 11 A.M., heading southeast. He'd be on it.

He packed his few belongings into a carpetbag, then attached the makeshift sling he'd constructed for his Winchester and slung it over his shoulder. He'd picked up the idea of the sling from his army days; when the gun was over your shoulder it left both hands free, but was near it if it was needed.

Spur next stopped by the livery stable to make sure his roan would be well cared for during his absence. The animal snorted her disapproval at Spur, and stamped her front right hoof twice, so he went to the animal and rubbed her snout.

"You gonna be gone long?" the liveryman asked.

"Don't know. At least a week, maybe two. Depends on how long it takes."

"You going there on business?" The man's Irish accent overpowered his words. He looked up from where he was hanging Spur's saddle on the wall.

Spur gave him a cold look. The man shrugged his apology for the question. "Don't worry; I'll take good care of her," he said, walking back to smooth down the roan's mane.

"You do that. See you in a couple of weeks." Spur went to the depot, bought a ticket to Fargo, and sat on the hard wooden bench outside the waiting room.

The sun was up, but the air was still cold. Spur settled back on the bench, removed his bag of fixings from his shirt pocket and rolled a smoke. As he lit it and inhaled he heard the faint but unmistakeable sound of a sixgun cocking behind him.

Spur threw the smoke down and whirled, his Colt already drawn, trigger finger ready, as he wondered who had drawn on him.

THREE

An instant after he saw the man Spur dived to his right. A slug slammed through the back of the bench, splintering the wood. Spur took quick aim on the man and squeezed off a shot that set the sixgun flying. The bushwhacker grabbed his hand, then stared at Spur in unconcealed hatred.

"Bastard!" he said.

Spur rose to his feet, keeping the man covered. "Who are you? And why are you trying to spoil my day?"

The man wiped his forehead. He was caked with grime, mud and dust, and sweat beaded on his face. He looked as if he'd slept under the stars more than he had under a roof; it showed in the deep-brown finish of his sun-leathered skin.

"Carter," the man said. "The name's Carter. And I should've killed you, after what you done."

Spur was sure he'd never met the man, but sometimes his memory wasn't good enough to recollect every man he'd put behind bars or chased out of town. "I've never seen you before, have I?"

"Maybe not. But I seen you. You remember that shack out back of Rocky Creek?"

"Sure. I was there yesterday rounding up some gold thieves."

"Yeah, well, I was one of them you didn't round up."

"You don't say."

"That's right."

"So why the hell are you here? You want to get yourself killed?"

"I got some unfinished business with you."

Spur snorted. "Christ, boy, I'm leaving town and won't be back for a while. You could have laid low and waited until I'd cleared out, and not had anything to worry about."

"That ain't good enough for me, Spur," the man said. "You killed my friends. You stole our gold."

"It wasn't your gold. It was United States government property."

"Horseshit it was! It was ours, and you had to butt in and fuck up our plans! Well, that's the last time you'll do that."

"All right, Carter; since you're so fired up to see your friends again, let's walk down to the sheriff's."

"Nothing doing," the man said, smiling.

"Why not?"

" 'Cause I don't wanna go." The man stole a glance at his gun; it lay on the platform ten feet away.

Spur followed his gaze for an instant and then was sorry for having done it; when he turned back to Carter the man was aiming a tiny wicked derringer. Spur fired first, his slug puncturing Carter's chest.

24

The man looked surprised for a moment before slumping to the platform.

Spur stood and watched as the man died. A thin pool of blood formed around his body as the sheriff ran up, along with several other men and women.

"What the hell happened here, Spur?" the sheriff asked, his eye twitching.

"His name's Carter. He was with the gang who stole the gold I recovered two days ago. I just finished my job."

"You mean he was the other one, the one who got away?"

"That's right. But how'd you know? I didn't have any idea anyone got away."

"I didn't know for sure," the sheriff said. "As we were riding up, the posse and I saw a rider high-tailin' it away from Rocky Creek. We figured it might be one of the gang but didn't stop to find out. We had to get there to save your ass."

Spur smiled, then nodded. "I see. I just wish you'd told me about him. I would have been prepared."

"Looks like you handled him just fine, Spur." The sheriff turned and frowned at the crowd that had gathered near the railroad platform. "All right, folks, the show's over. Go about your business." He glanced at the body, then up at Spur. "You leaving?"

"Yeah. Leaving."

"Spur, you can't even leave town without causing a fuss. Well, good luck, wherever you're going, though I doubt you'll need it." The sheriff smiled and slapped Spur's back.

"Thanks, Sheriff. Will you take care of this?" Spur pointed to Carter's body.

"Sure. Don't worry about it. Self-defense, of course. And you being who you are, there won't be any trouble. No reason why you can't leave town."

"I appreciate that, Sheriff."

"It's all I can do after you got the gold back. Stay in one piece, Spur."

"I'll sure as hell try, Sheriff; I'll sure as hell try."

Two deputies picked up Carter's body and carried him away. Soon Spur was alone on the platform, waiting for the eastbound train.

He made the trip to Fargo with no problems. Not long ago the journey would have taken a week by horseback; now with the great "iron horses" it could be done in less than a day. Times were changing.

Carrying his carpetbag, toting his Winchester repeater, and packing his Colt .44 on his hip, Spur walked along the streets of Fargo. It was a growing town; he could tell by the new buildings that lined the streets and the citified faces he saw on many of the townsfolk. Transplants from back east, Spur thought, as he nodded to a family. The woman, her face pinched, looked at Spur's firearms and hustled her children away from him. He smiled, tipped his wide-brimmed hat to her, and continued on his way to find a hotel.

He stopped at the first one he came to. He was sure there were more, but since he had no way of knowing which was better or worse, he might as well take the closest one and save the walk. Spur entered through the double doors and came to a halt. The aroma of fried fish, beans and coffee filled the lobby. Realizing he was hungry, he dumped his carpetbag on the hardwood floor.

"Anyone here?" he called.

"Yes, I'm in here," a feminine voice said from his right. "If you want a room, come in and get some food. If you're here on some other business, have a seat and I'll be out in a minute."

Spur smiled, laid his rifle next to the carpetbag, and walked in through a narrow door into a kitchen. A young woman, her blonde hair tied high on her head, wearing a gingham dress covered by a stained apron, bent over a wood-burning stove and picked up a pot of coffee.

As she gripped the wooden handle she looked up and saw him, smiled, and set the pot down.

"Hello," she said, wiping her hands on the apron.

"Hi. Got a spare room?"

"Sure. Fact is, I've got plenty. Business is slow this time of year." Her face, devoid of artificial aids, was vibrantly beautiful; the eyes clear blue, the cheeks high and firm, the lips full and sensuous. Under the apron Spur saw the outlines of a firm youthful body. She couldn't be over twenty-five, he decided.

The woman didn't seem to notice his reverie, and Spur realized she was in one of her own. Her eyes surveyed his face, dropped to his feet, then raised to his crotch and lingered there for a moment before returning to look into his eyes.

"So I've got a room for you. Are you new in town?"

"Yes," Spur said, not giving her any details.

27

"You hungry? I've got plenty of food. I always make up extra in case I get a customer."

Spur looked at the pots and skillet that simmered and sizzled on the stove behind her.

"Sure am."

"Then sit down and I'll feed you." She motioned to the ten-foot-long plain wooden table that ran the length of the huge kitchen. Spur nodded and sat.

The woman put a plate in front of him, loaded it with fresh-fried catfish, then dumped on a pile of simmered beans. Finally she filled a heavy mug with coffee and set that down before him.

"Anything else?" she asked, filling her own cup.

"Do I have to eat with my fingers?" Spur asked.

The woman looked at the table, then shook her head and smiled. "I'm sorry. I'm not used to this yet." She stood and collected a knife and fork, then handed them to him and sat opposite him.

"You're new in the hotel business, then?" The building did have a fresh, clean look to it.

"Yes. Well, actually no. I mean—well, it's hard to explain." Her face had a confused, frustrated expression. "Sometimes I wish I'd never started this place up again after Daddy died."

"Your father owned the hotel?"

"Not this one—another, that he sold when he got sick. He died just this past spring. I didn't know what to do, so I decided to go into his business."

"How's it been so far?"

"I'd rather not talk about that. It was a shambles from the start. First there was the problem with the loan. I don't know why I had so much trouble; Mr. Drucker's known me all my life, practically."

"He your banker?"

"That's right. Then, after I got the money from him, I had trouble finding labor and the men I did hire fell behind. It turned out two men from San Francisco had decided to open a fancy hotel here in Fargo, on the other side of town, and they had the best men working on it. It's called the Drake and Mason. So when I finally got this hotel open they'd already attracted a lot of attention and caught most of the customers. Some writer from New York stayed there and wrote about it in the papers and now the Drake and Mason is getting customers from the East."

"Business will pick up," Spur said. "After all, I'm staying here now."

"That's right." Her mood lightened. "I'm grateful to you, Mr. . . . ."

"Mr. McCoy. But I don't see how I can keep this place open much longer if I don't get more business."

"A beautiful woman like you couldn't have too much bad luck."

She smiled brightly. "You do have a way of cheering me up."

Spur finished his dinner and drank the rest of the coffee. "Best supper I've had in a long time," he said.

"Kind of you to say so. I'm so used to my own cooking I barely notice it any more. You'll be wanting to see your room now, right?"

"Sure. Whatever you want."

She smiled deliciously. "Well, if that was the case I might take you to my room." She paused, then

29

went on. "Does that shock you, Mr. McCoy?"

"No. I like a woman who speaks her mind. Saves a lot of time that way, usually." Was the woman actually asking him to share her bed with her?

"Well, Mr. McCoy, which room do you want to see first? Yours or mine?"

He shrugged. "You're the lady of the house. Why don't you decide?" But as he looked at her, Spur felt the old desire building up.

The woman removed her apron, unpinned her hair, and then, after it had cascaded past her shoulders, threw her head back and reached for his hand. "Follow me."

They walked from the kitchen across the front lobby, where she paused momentarily to lock the entrance, then to a door near the fireplace. She opened it and went in.

Spur followed. It was a woman's room, with a frilly four-poster bed and a vase of flowers on the dresser.

"Mr. McCoy, this is my room."

"Very nice," Spur said, and shut the door behind him.

The woman ran across the room and wrapped her arms around him. "Oh, Mr. McCoy, it's been so long . . . so very long!"

Spur removed his hat and kissed her forehead. "Hey, take it easy. We've got time. Besides, I don't even know your name."

"Julie. Julie Wyler. That's why I named this place the Wyler Hotel." She reached for his flannel shirt and began unbuttoning it. When she had the front opened she ran her hands down his chest, her fingers

30

gently pulling at the hairs there.

Spur smiled. Until that moment he hadn't known how serious the woman was. Now it was plain. She wanted to be stripped, thrown onto the bed and ridden like a horse. He caught her head in his hands and pushed his mouth down onto hers. Spur probed with his tongue, and she instantly opened her lips to let it glide in, while her hands worked down his chest until they came to rest on the hard lump between his legs. He broke the kiss and she gasped, rubbing his erection.

"Hurry and get your clothes off!" Her face was flushed a bright pink as she moved her hands to unbutton her dress.

Just after Spur had pulled off his shirt they both heard gunfire and screams from outside. Spur bent to look out the window. Julie pushed in beside him.

"My God!" she said.

Black smoke climbed into the sky two blocks down Main Street. They heard more gunfire and screams as the smoke continued to fill the air.

"The raiders!" Julie said. "I'll bet it's the raiders again!"

"What raiders?" Spur asked.

"Never mind. Come on. We better go see if we can help. Damnit, why now?" She buttoned her dress while Spur threw on his shirt. In seconds they were out of the hotel and had joined the crown running toward the smoke-belching building.

Spur cursed the raiders' timing; it couldn't have been worse.

31

FOUR

Spur and Julie stopped and stared at the angry orange and red flames that licked the huge beautiful building. Men jumped from windows, coughing and sputtering, their faces blackened. There were no signs of the raiders; they must have already left. They had been quick.

Spur saw a sign above the doors: "Drake and Mason's New Hotel." The paint on the sign peeled and boiled in the heat, and a moment later was totally consumed in flames.

A dozen men had formed a bucket brigade, throwing pails of water onto the fire in a futile attempt to put it out. Spur looked at Julie, then joined the effort, but the heat grew so intense that they had to back away. A minor explosion ripped through the building and stopped the brigade. Windows blew out, raining shattered glass onto the street.

Spur returned to Julie, who stood staring at the flames. After a moment she looked down at the ground. Her eyes riveted onto the three charred and smoking bodies, lying where they had been pulled from the fire. She screamed and buried her face on Spur's chest, and he held her while the building collapsed onto itself and sent flames shooting fifty feet into the air.

Around them, men, women and children stared; some cried, others watched in wonder, but most betrayed their inner anger by small gestures: clenched teeth, a fist, a shuffle in the dirt.

"It's time something was done about those raiders," Spur heard one man near him say.

"Yeah, but what's a man to do? The sheriff's done everything he can. There's no way he can do more. There's nothing nobody can do, as far as I can tell."

Spur listened to the man intently. He had to keep a low profile; it would look suspicious if he hurried around asking questions about the fire. If he listened to the conversations around him he could learn much.

"Something should be done," another man said. "This is going too far. Much too far."

"Time was when they was just botherin' folks; now they're killing them. I wonder if anyone we know's a raider?"

"Shut your mouth, Frazer!" the first man said. "Don't even talk like that."

"I just meant—"

"I know what you meant, but that kind of talk could get both of us killed. Come on; I'm having a drink. I need one."

"Yeah, me too."

The voices trailed off as the men walked from the area.

Spur held Julie's hand, squeezing it when she looked up at him. He turned to the man next to him and cleared his throat. After he had caught the man's attention, Spur spoke.

"You know what started it?"

The man's face in the firelight was brownish-red, tanned, deeply lined. The eyes were habitually suspicious, the mouth tight and reluctant.

"Don't know."

"It was the raiders, wasn't it?" Spur prodded.

"Could be."

The man wasn't offering any information.

"What do you mean, 'could be'? Everyone around here says it was them. What're you trying to hide, old man?"

"Nothing. I don't talk about them people." He turned and walked from Spur with a limp, his back straight despite his years.

"Spur," Julie said. "Let's go back. I can't stand this smoke."

"I've got to stay to see if I can be some help," Spur said. "You go on ahead. I'll see you later."

Julie nodded. "All right." She turned and left for her hotel.

Spur watched Julie go, then shifted his attention to the fire. It had nearly burned itself out; huge timbers glowed like sunlit rubies. Smoke drifted up from a thousand charred splinters as the last flames flickered out.

The crowd that had gathered before the building dispersed. Spur followed a pack of men to Kelly's Saloon, went to the bar and ordered a rye whiskey.

He picked it up, swallowed the warm liquid and felt it travel to his stomach. He turned to the man

35

next to him.

"You see the fire?" Spur asked.

"Yeah. Awful thing." The face, blackened with smoke, was covered with a sheen of perspiration, which the man continually wiped at with the back of his hand. It was a young face, but worn out by worry and work. His hand trembled as he lifted his glass.

"You know what went on?" Spur asked.

"Hell, not really. Just what I heard from some of the others. Someone set it; that's a fact. It was the raiders, of course; it's always the raiders!" He swallowed and coughed.

For a moment Spur thought he saw a tear in the man's eye, but he turned his head and ordered another drink.

"Clyde Riley the other day. And now Drake and Mason and his wife." He shook his head. "Fargo's coming to an end. Those raiders'll kill as many as they can and drive out the rest. But for what? What are they gaining from it?"

"Clyde Riley?"

The man turned to Spur. "Yeah. Rontrell and his raiders went out to Riley's ranch the other day early in the morning; they killed him, roughed up his wife and left. Now I hear Mary's thinking about moving; she can't manage the ranch herself. I think she's also afraid of another attack from Rontrell and his raiders."

"Rontrell's the leader?" Spur asked casually.

The man shot him a glance. "Say, why're you so goddamned interested in all this?"

"Just makin' conversation," Spur said smoothly.

36

"I'm from out of town, don't know what's happening." He gripped his glass and swirled the contents.

"Well, all right. Yeah, Rontrell's the leader —that's the talk around town, at least. I don't know who started calling him Rontrell, but someone did and the name stuck. No one knows his real name."

"How long have these attacks been going on?"

"Two months, maybe longer. At first they were small things—setting a privy on fire, breaking windows, stampeding cattle. That type. Then they began bothering people—a couple of men I know got beat up real bad one night walking home from the saloon. And I came back one day to find Emma—my wife—tied to the bed, all the dishes broke, the front door torn off. I don't know why; I've never done nothin' to nobody!"

"And now Clyde Riley's been killed and the hotel's been burned."

"Yeah, with Lance Drake, Bill Mason and Esther—Mason's wife—in it. I just can't believe it's gone this far."

"What about the sheriff?" Spur said, lowering his voice.

"Mel tries, but how much can you do when you don't know who's responsible, and when they come and go like lightning? That and those damned masks they always wear; you can't tell who they are."

"Have you ever seen the raiders?"

"Sure, a couple of times."

"Could you identify any of the men? I know they wear masks, but what about their boots? A certain type of clothing? Or even their horses?"

The man shook his head. "It always happens so fast; one minute they're there, then they're gone. I never have time to see anything; I'm usually too busy running." The man pulled at a beer. "I hope I never see those bastards again, but every time I go out I look over my shoulder, expecting to find a masked man starin' at me, his finger on a trigger."

"Thanks for the talk," Spur said. He drained his glass and walked through the saloon, but didn't make it to the batwing doors before a raven-haired beauty in a green dress tapped him on the shoulder.

"My name's Lila," she said. "Can I buy you a drink?"

"No thanks," Spur said. "Have to be going."

She shrugged. "Okay. Maybe later." She sauntered away.

Spur smiled at the saloon girl and walked out the doors.

After renting a room from Julie at Wyler's Hotel and getting a good rest, Spur was up at dawn. He broke down both his Winchester and his Colt, cleaned and oiled them, and reassembled each before he went downstairs to eat.

At eight Spur rented a fine bay horse at the livery and rode off for Clyde Riley's ranch. The directions he'd received from Julie indicated it lay an hour's ride out of Fargo to the north.

When the ranch came into view, Spur halted his horse and looked at it. It was small, and practically identical with thousands of others scattered throughout the west: an ill-constructed barn, a pair of corrals and a small squat house.

He touched his spurs to the horse's flanks and in less than ten minutes was close to the front door.

Just as Spur was preparing to dismount a slug slammed into the earth inches from his horse's hooves. The animal neighed but remained still. Spur jerked it to the left and dropped to his feet, then slid behind it. The shot had come from the house.

FIVE

Spur strained his eyes but couldn't see whether the front door to Mary Riley's ranch house was open; he was sure that was where the shot had come from, but he couldn't see a gun barrel there.

"You just get out of here!" a strong woman's voice said. "You raiders have hurt me enough! If you don't leave this minute I'll shoot to kill."

Spur almost smiled. He moved, but then heard a slug fly past his shoulder. "No!" he yelled, ducking. "Wait a minute, Mrs. Riley. I'm not a raider!"

"The hell you ain't."

"I'm not wearing a mask, am I?"

"You're just trying to fool me," the unseen woman said.

"I'm here to ask you some questions."

"What kind of questions?"

"About the raiders."

Silence. The door opened inward, and Spur saw a young, strikingly beautiful woman step through it to the front porch. She kept her rifle trained on Spur as he stood and approached her.

"I'm glad you decided to stop shooting," he said lightly.

"A woman can't be too careful." She studied him intently. "Who are you and what did you say you wanted?"

"I'm Spur McCoy, and I'd like to know as much about the raiders as you can tell me, Mrs. Riley."

Spur was surprised at the woman's beauty. Outdoor living and hard work hadn't toughened her skin or decreased her attractiveness; the face was still light complexioned, the eyes clear, with no wrinkles around them, and from what Spur could see beneath her gingham dress her body was firm and slender.

"Why do you want to know about them?" Mrs. Riley asked.

"Do you think you could lower your rifle?" Spur asked. "I can't talk with one of those in my face."

"What? Oh, I'm sorry." She dropped it to her side, then smiled. "Why don't you come inside, Mr. McCoy. I guess I can trust you."

"That'd be fine."

He followed her into the house and to a chair next to a smoky, sputtering fire.

"I don't know much about the raiders myself," she said, when they were seated. "Just what I saw and heard."

"That's what I'd like to know."

"Well, they came early in the morning. It was this tall man—Rontrell, everyone calls him—and five others. Rontrell said that Clyde had killed a woman and her children three years ago in Missouri, and that he deserved to die. I think it had something to do with the army—I mean, that's what Rontrell said. He also told Clyde that he was doing justice, like he was some kind of sheriff or something.''

"And?''

"And then he killed Clyde. Tied him to the back porch and shot him. That's all. They rode away.''

"But Clyde hadn't done anything like that,'' Spur said.

She looked up quickly. "No. Clyde never wore a sixgun; he hated them. It was in the war that he started hating them; apparently when he was a kid he used to shoot up everything he saw, but the war turned him against the things completely.'' She looked at the rifle that she still held, then leaned it against the stone wall. "Now he won't wear a gun—I mean, he wouldn't.''

"But this Rontrell was convinced that Clyde had killed a woman and her two children?''

"Yes. That's what he said. I suppose he thought that gave him the right to kill Clyde; and maybe he really did believe it. I don't know, Mr. McCoy. I really don't. All I do know is that I'm tired and scared. I'm moving out of here as soon as I can afford it.''

"Where are you going?''

"Denver, for starters. I don't know what I'll do. I might go back to New York. I can't say for sure yet. There's nothing for me here now, with Clyde gone.''

"I see. Mrs. Riley, did you notice anything out of the way about any of the raiders? I realize they were all masked, but was there a certain horse, or perhaps a piece of clothing, that you remember?''

After a second she shook her head firmly. "No. I

43

was too frightened, angry and bewildered to be noticing anything of that nature. I'm sorry I can't be of more help, Mr. McCoy. I'm just not good at these things. And I've already answered the sheriff's questions." She looked at him in perfect seriousness. "I don't know why you want to know all this, but leave the raiders alone. There's nothing you can do; there's nothing anybody can do. The sheriff has tried and failed; he lost a deputy during a raid not more than two weeks ago. No—stay out of it, Mr. McCoy, for your own sake."

"I appreciate the advice."

"But you'll ignore it?"

"Mrs. Riley, would you be kind enough not to mention that I was out to see you today?"

"Why?"

"I'd appreciate it," Spur said, and looked into her eyes.

"Okay. I'm sure you have your reasons. I'll be gone within the week so I don't suppose I'll have cause to tell anyone. I hope I've been some help, Mr. McCoy."

They rose.

"You have, and thanks."

She smiled and walked him to the door. Spur swung up onto the saddle and started back to Fargo. Mrs. Riley hadn't been much help. But her revelations that Rontrell had accused her husband of the murder of a woman and her two children made him think.

Was Rontrell satisfying some kind of urge for revenge? If so, how could it possibly be connected with the people of Fargo?

Maybe Rontrell had thought that Clyde Riley had killed those people, and he was doing justice. But that didn't explain the others he'd killed—not unless they too had committed crimes in their past that Rontrell had stumbled across.

The horse gently trotted back to town. Mary Riley had complicated matters further, but now at least he had some more facts to work with.

As Spur rounded a large stand of trees he heard the splat of a rifle bullet slam into a young oak six feet to his right, and a few seconds later the sharp crack of the rifle somewhere ahead of him. A damn bushwhacker.

Spur swung off his horse, ran it into the trees, and stood behind one of the thicker oaks. Silence. He watched the area from which he believed the shot had come. It was flat, with few trees, a small, shrub-covered rise arching out of the area, topped with three gray boulders. The gunman must be there.

Spur's Colt was useless at that range. He had to move closer. He glanced at the horse; it was chewing peacefully on a rich patch of grass. It would stay there. He jumped from tree to tree, watching the rocks on the rise, zigzagging to the left and then the right, gaining four to six feet each time. Spur reached the last of the trees; he was still more than forty feet from the foot of the rise, farther from where the gunman must lay.

He had three choices, Spur knew; he could wait out the gunman, attempt a direct attack on the boulders, or circle around back. Spur chose the latter; it seemed the safest.

He broke from the cover of the trees, hunched

45

down, moving across the open area. He didn't want to fire. The gunman must think he was still in the trees.

Spur moved faster, trying to reach a small patch of shrubs that looked to be practically in line with the boulders. From there he should be able to see his enemy. His knees aching, he cleared the last ten feet and quietly moved into the brush, which he now recognized as a nearly solid mass of sunflowers, their seed-filled heads nodding to the ground, dry, browned. Spur pushed one stem from his face and peered at the boulders. A man sat there reloading his rifle. He wore a mask that covered the lower half of his face.

A raider? Somehow they already knew about him. Or perhaps the man was using him for target practice. Either way, Spur wasn't happy; if the raiders knew Spur's purpose for his presence in Fargo it would make his job a hell of a lot tougher.

Still too far from the man for an accurate shot, Spur settled back on his haunches and waited for him to finish reloading and take another shot at the trees. Then his back would be to Spur, and it wouldn't take much time to run closer, where he could get off two or three shots at the man. He'd have only one chance; if he missed, the man would turn and use the rifle.

The raider seemed to be in no hurry; when he had finished loading he leisurely inspected his rifle, as if he had time to spare. That didn't make sense unless he realized that Spur had been too far from him to return his fire effectively. Apparently the man had blundered; he should have waited until Spur was closer to him before he took the first shot. But it was too late now.

Damnit, Spur said to himself. He couldn't move without being seen while the man was turned this way; in fact Spur was surprised he hadn't been seen so far. The man must assume Spur was still in the trees.

Just as Spur's knees were getting uncomfortable from squatting in the sunflowers, the gunman surprised him by rising and moving down the back of the rise. In an instant he was out of sight.

He's probably going to try and flush me out of the woods, Spur thought. The rifleman must be circling around the same way Spur had done.

Spur rose and walked to the base of the rise, then carefully moved around it, searching for the raider. Finally the trees were in sight; the bushwhacker was just entering them. Spur walked beside the man's mount and then dashed across the open space and moved into the woods. He searched every shadow, every trunk. Nothing. The man wasn't there.

A second later Spur heard the neigh of a horse behind him; the rifleman had mounted and was heading out of the area. He must have assumed Spur was gone; but surely he'd seen Spur's mount? Maybe he'd tired of the game. Either way, he'd left Spur standing among the oaks, watching him ride off.

Spur almost took a shot at the departing raider but decided against it; he didn't want to betray his presence in case the man figured he had left. At least he knew the horse; the raider's mount was white with deep brown spots, no bigger than eyes, covering it. If he saw the horse in town Spur would watch who claimed it; then he'd have identified his first raider.

He went back to his own horse and rode to Fargo. On the way he kept his eyes open for the rifleman, but he ran into no trouble.

SIX

Clint Johnson poured brandy into a snifter, replaced the decanter on the rack, and settled his six-foot frame into his chair, watching the flames crackle and spark behind the peacock-shaped brass fire-screen. His smooth, unlined face was relaxed and calm; the neatly trimmed sideburns and dusty brown beard matched the color of his eyes and of his longish hair. At thirty-five his body was slim and well built.

In his study, Johnson relaxed, worked out problems, let the pretensions and facades fall. It was the sole place in which he could do so; therefore it was his refuge, his hideout.

Johnson looked into the flames and momentarily saw Clyde Riley's face as it had looked just before he died. The memory caused laughter to rise in him but he quickly quelled it. That bastard had been scared, and rightly so. He knew he was guilty and had to pay the ultimate price when justice found him and demanded settlement. That Clint Johnson had been the instrument of justice wasn't important; it could have been anyone, but he'd taken the responsibility upon himself.

He turned to the window. His plan was working. The town was in an uproar. After sundown the streets were bereft of all but the most hardened gunmen. Normally wary men had become gun-happy maniacs, shooting at shadows and occasionally at each other, always watching for the raiders.

They were side effects, but they were acceptable to Johnson. He wanted the town to be gripped by fear. Those who were innocent would be spared; those who weren't would receive their punishment.

Fortunately, he'd received the help and cooperation of Fargo's leaders. There was one man more to be destroyed or brought to his thinking; he'd resisted all attempts to the present, but Johnson would bring him around or have the man killed. Nothing would stand in his way.

The door to his study burst open, disturbing his thoughts. A paunchy, sweating man walked in, his fleshy face flushed with excitement, his neck jiggling above the collar of his dress shirt and vest.

Rontrell rose to his feet.

"What the hell are you doing here, Zane?" He threw the snifter onto the floor—where it shattered—then glared at the man.

"Sorry, Mr.—"

"I don't care to hear any of your explanations," Johnson thundered, striding across the floor to the man.

"But Mr. Johnson, we've got trouble."

He stopped. "What kind of trouble? Be specific, Zane!"

"It's that new man in town—ah, Spur McCoy, the one you had watched. Sure enough he rode out to Mary Riley's place this morning. He spent about half an hour there, then rode back."

"Anything else?"

"Yes. Jim was following him, like you told him to. He took a few shots at Spur but missed him; the next thing he knew McCoy had up and left."

Johnson stared at the corpulent man. "It would have been pleasant to have the man dead. Of course, I don't know for sure that he's here to investigate us, but it smells that way." Johnson looked at the spray of glass on the floor, then back up to the man. "I don't quite know what to do with Spur."

"Should I have him killed?" Zane asked. "It wouldn't be too hard. I'll put a better shot on him."

"And risk missing him again?" Johnson shook his head. "No, we can't afford that. Anyway, if Mr. McCoy is working for the state government in some way we wouldn't want his death to bring state attention to Fargo. Kill Spur and we might get two or three more like him. No, we can't risk that. Have him watched, Zane, but try to ensure that he doesn't know he's being watched."

"I surely will," he said. "Anything else?"

"Yes. We'll have a meeting tonight."

"Everyone, or just the main men?"

"Better leave it to the key men; I don't want the screaming masses to know what I've got in store for them. Not yet."

Zane's eyes grew narrow. "You're planning something special, Mr. Johnson?"

"Yes, but I can't talk about it now. Have the signal flag put out this afternoon, and pass the word

51

as best you can. I'm not going to let Spur put a dent in my plans—not yet, at any rate. He can't hurt us now. But if he gets too close, the rules still follow—have him killed. I don't want him meddling with us. Is that clear, Zane?''

"Yes, Mr. Johnson. It is. It surely is.'' He frowned. "And I'm sorry about barging in, Mr. Johnson. It's just that I couldn't wait to tell you the news.''

"I understand, but at least knock the next time, will you? You had no idea of what I was doing in here. I could have had a lady with me.''

Zane grinned. "That you could have, Mr. Johnson. There ain't a woman in town you couldn't have, if you put your mind to it. Lila Fairley, for instance. I bet you could have her dress off in less than a minute if you put your mind to it.''

"Yes, I suppose I could,'' Johnson said, a sly smile playing about his lips. "As a matter of fact I've often thought of taking Lila to my bed. I know she wouldn't dare refuse me. But never mind, Zane. You'd better get on with your work, and I with mine. Oh, and find Jim and tell him not to kill Spur.''

"I'll try, but it might be hard, Mr. Johnson. He told me what happened, then left. I don't know where.''

"Find him, you hear me? Or I'll hold you personally responsible. I don't want anything to happen to Spur McCoy—not yet.''

"I'll try, Mr. Rontrell. I better get going and find Jim. I hope he hasn't done anything foolish.''

"I hope not too. For your sake.''

Zane nodded nervously and exited.

Spur McCoy was the only dark spot on his plan, the only fly in the ointment that could jeopardize the batch. Johnson must go slow on McCoy, not wanting to attract any outside attention—but if he had to, he'd have the man killed and buried.

Johnson looked down at the shattered snifter, then shrugged. He'd have to call the maid to clean it up. That was no problem. Spur McCoy wasn't much different. If the man didn't watch his step, Rontrell would simply call one of his men to "clean him up."

He looked at the dying fire, shook his head, and bent to add fresh fuel. As the flames lapped higher, he backed away, smiling, thinking of how well his plan was going.

Soon. Soon he would have his full satisfaction, and the screams that resounded in his mind every waking hour would be stilled forever.

SEVEN

Spur closed his hotel-room door, bent and leaned a
splinter of wood against the bottom of it. After the
bushwhacker in the trees he had to be careful. If the
splinter was gone when he returned, or had fallen,
he'd know someone had been in his room.

He went to Kelly's and drank two whiskeys while
questioning several men about the raiders. None
would talk to him openly, and from what Spur knew
about the raiders he wasn't surprised. Several times
he felt someone looking at him, and finally found the
source of his discomfort—a pretty lady with jet-
black hair and a green dress sitting at a small table
in the corner of the saloon.

After the sixth man had turned from him, refusing
to answer his questions, Spur went to the woman
and recognized her as the one who'd introduced
herself yesterday.

"Hello, Lila," Spur said, and sat.

"Hi yourself, Spur McCoy. You looking for some
information?"

"Yeah."

"I could tell you something about the raiders."
Her eyes were dark and flashing, and up close she
was pretty enough to make a preacher stand up at
attention when she walked into a room, Spur
thought. He caught the scent of her perfume as she
leaned to him across the table.

"But it's going to cost you. Think you might like
to try your luck at a game of blackjack?"

"Sure. But what about the raiders?"

"Later. After I win the pants off you." She
laughed and shuffled the cards.

"How much are you willing to lose to me?" Spur
asked, watching her expertly manipulate the cards.

"Enough." Lila stopped and laid her purse on the
table while Spur fished in his pockets and came up
with five silver dollars.

He set one in the center of the table and Lila dealt.
Spur looked at his face-down cards; ace of spades
and the two of hearts. He frowned and glanced at
Lila's top-facing card—ten of diamonds.

"Hit me," Spur said.

Five of clubs. Eighteen or eight.

"Any more?" she asked.

Spur shook his head.

"Dealer hits." She dealt herself the two of
diamonds and laid it against the ten, then turned
over the hole card to show the seven of hearts.

"Nineteen."

Spur shrugged and moved the silver dollar and
cards to her. She shuffled as Spur pushed another
dollar onto the table. He received the seven of
diamonds and the queen of hearts by the deal.

"Hit me," Spur said, with all the confidence of a

riverboat gambler. It was only a dollar, after all.

She peeled off a card and laid it before him. Four of clubs.

"Another?" Lila asked.

"No. Twenty-one. I win."

"Easy come, easy go," Lila said, and handed him a dollar from her purse.

Spur took the cards. As he shuffled he wondered who Lila Fairley was. She didn't seem the saloon-girl type, but she was sitting in Kelly's playing blackjack with a stranger. He shrugged and dealt after she had placed her bet in the center of the table.

His cards were the five of spades and the queen of clubs. Lila looked at her cards and pursed her lips momentarily, then glanced at Spur.

"Hit me."

Jack of diamonds.

"Again."

Ace of hearts.

"That's fine."

Spur turned up the queen.

"Dealer hits."

He dealt himself the two of hearts, then the four of clubs.

"Twenty-one."

Lila pushed her cards and money to him.

"Maybe you're better than I thought, Mr. McCoy. That was nearly the last of my money, and I don't get paid until tomorrow."

"You want to quit?"

"No. I've still got one more thing to bet." She reached under the table and seconds later dropped a lacy black garter onto the table.

He smiled and dealt. A six of diamonds showed in his hand, with his hole card a one-eyed jack.

"Want a card?" he asked.

"Yes."

He gave her one, then another. Lila had eleven showing. "That's enough."

Spur dealt himself a four. "Twenty-one," he said, turning over his other cards.

Lila shrugged and handed her garter to Spur.

"That's that. You won me for the day. What will you do with me, Spur?" A smile lit up her face.

"How about answering some questions about the raiders?"

She shrugged. "That's fine . . . for a start. But not here. It's too public. Let's go to my place."

"All right." They rose as a handsome man in his midthirties, dressed in a black suit, string tie and half boots, walked up to them.

"Lila Fairley, I've been meaning to talk with you."

"Mr. Johnson, I haven't seen you lately. Where've you been hiding?"

"I've been busy." He turned to Spur. "I don't think I've met this gentleman." The man took a hard look at Spur, and McCoy returned the favor. He was near his prime; he moved like a cat, his eyes sharp and clear, his skin tanned and wrinkle free.

"Spur McCoy," the Secret Service man said, extending his hand.

The other man clasped it and smiled. "Clint Johnson. You new in town, Mr. McCoy?"

"Yes, just in yesterday. Not long before the fire

58

broke out."

The man's eyes fell. "Yes. Tragic. I couldn't believe it, that beautiful new place up in flames in seconds."

"Did you want to talk with me?" Lila asked, interrupting.

"Yes, but seeing as how you've got company, it can wait. Perhaps tomorrow, Miss Fairley?"

"That'd be fine, Mr. Johnson."

"Good. Well, Mr. McCoy, I'm sure I'll be seeing you again. Welcome to Fargo, and I hope you'll enjoy your stay here."

"I'm sure I will."

The man smiled shortly and walked away. When he was out of sight Lila grabbed Spur's arm and led him, without a word, out of the saloon. They walked down Main Street until they halted before a small squat structure—a boarding house, Spur thought.

They went inside and up a flight of stairs, then into a room. When Lila had the door closed and had turned up the flame on the kerosene lamps, she turned to him and sighed.

"Whew. I'm glad to be out of that man's company."

"You mean Clint Johnson?"

"Yes."

"He seems a decent enough man."

"Sure, to you. But he's been trying to get me into his bed ever since he moved here three years ago." She stopped and smiled. "I don't mince words, Mr. McCoy. I hope that doesn't bother you."

"It doesn't."

"Good. It's just that he's asked me more than

once and I've always said no. It irritates me. I'll bet that's what he wanted to ask me."

"What does he do in Fargo?"

"Nothing. He's rich—loads of money. Owns a few gold mines in Colorado, from what I hear, and some of Fargo itself." She sat on the bed and bent to remove her shoes.

"Hmmmm. But you don't like him?" He leaned against the door, arms on his chest, watching her.

"No. But let's not talk about that. Ahh, that feels better." She wriggled her feet and set the shoes next to the dresser. "The only thing he cares about is money. He could even be mixed up with some outlaws. All I've got is my suspicions, though."

"Ever talk to anybody else about him?"

"No. That's why I cleared you out of the saloon before I talked to you about him." She looked at him frankly. "Of course, that wasn't the only reason. I hope you don't think I'm too bold for bringing you to my room."

"Why should I?"

"Some men think a woman shouldn't act that way. I mean, well, a woman who knows what she wants and doesn't mind talking about it."

"You mean some of the men of Fargo?"

She nodded. "I guess I don't have the best reputation in town, but I don't care. I really don't! As long as they leave me alone they can say whatever they want."

"I agree. It's nobody's business but mine what I do."

She smiled. "That's exactly the way I feel, Mr. McCoy." She paused. "Do you mind if I call you Spur?"

"You can call me anything you want."

"Good. Then you can call me Lila. I—I have to make a confession."

"What's that?"

"I saw you when you walked into the saloon yesterday, and I knew I had to meet you. And today I told you I'd talk about the raiders just to get you alone."

"Does that mean you won't discuss them?"

"No; I'll tell you everything I know. But I wonder why you're so interested in them."

"Does it really matter to you?" he asked quietly.

"Not really. As long as I can trust you not to go get yourself killed too quick by Rontrell and his raiders. But I do wish I knew what you were doing here. Especially if I'm going to help you."

"Let's not talk about it," Spur said. "There'll be plenty of time later."

"What should we do in the meantime?"

Spur caught the glint in her eyes then, the signal that she sent him. He walked to the bed and touched her left breast gently.

"How's this?"

"Wonderful. Just wonderful!" Lila grasped his hand and moved it to her other breast. "Oh Spur, I want you. Badly. Right now!"

She stood and he reached around to unbutton her dress while she sighed. Lila led her dress fall to the floor, then immodestly pulled off her chemise and petticoat and stepped out of the drawers. She stood naked before him.

Spur stared at her creamy white skin, her arching breasts with their dark areolas, her slender waist, and the gleaming patch of black hair between her legs.

Lila tugged at his pants. "Get that thing out!" she said. "I'm hornier than a hussy in August!"

Spur flipped his hat to the floor, ripped off his shirt, cursed his feet from his boots, then unbuttoned his pants and stepped from them.

While Lila saw him naked her eyes widened and she smiled broadly. "Spur, you're so big! I didn't think . . . I never thought. . . ."

"You don't have to think now," he said, and laid her down gently on the bed.

He climbed over her, then let his body press down onto hers. He ground his hips while he licked and gently bit her breasts. Lila moaned and shook her head from side to side as his mouth worked her over.

"Oh Spur, don't put me off! Get to the good stuff!"

He smiled and touched her legs. They parted and he raised himself, aimed and plunged inside her with one thrust. Lila's back arched and she closed her eyes as Spur began riding her. Her breath came in puffs and she moaned as Spur kissed her and pushed his tongue into her mouth.

He pulled his mouth from hers and slowed his driving hips. He was close, too close for his own enjoyment. He needed to slow down.

"Oh, don't stop!" she said. "I'm so close!"

"Don't worry," Spur said. "I'm not about to stop. I'm just saving it up for later."

With that he thrust harder and faster into her. Lila's sighs rang out constantly, and she pushed her hips up to meet his.

"Oh Spur, Spur—" Her words were cut off with a

short, sharp moan, then another, and finally she cried out.

Aroused by the woman's climax, Spur looked down at her bouncing breasts and flushed chest. He pounded even harder into her, and her moans again turned into cries. Spur slammed into Lila and let himself go while she writhed beneath him.

He sighed and collapsed on her body, his head beside hers, waiting for the room to stop shaking and the pounding in his ears to cease. Eventually he slid to his side and looked at her. Lila Fairley, her face flushed a bright pink, smiled at him and pulled a strand of hair from her eyes.

Spur felt his heart slow, his body recovering from the orgasm.

"Spur," Lila said, breaking the silence, "you do know how to treat a woman." She reached down and fondled him. "Would you treat me again?"

He smiled. "That wasn't enough?"

"It's never enough. I guess I'm what my father would call a loose woman."

"I've got a good cure for that."

Her hands coaxed him to fullness as his fingers traveled up and down the length of her body.

"All right," Lila said. "I'm ready again. But first . . . this is something I learned from a girlfriend of mine."

She bent and brought her head near his crotch, then snaked out her tongue and began licking the shaft. Spur tingled and a moment later pulled her head away.

"Damn!" he said.

"What?" She looked at him in surprise.

"I nearly lost it right there!"

"You never had a woman do that to you before?"

"Not often enough," he said with a smile. "It's almost more pleasure than a man can take."

"I'm glad you like it."

Spur grabbed her head and pulled it up from his crotch. "Not again. I don't want to disappoint you later. You just lie back and let me get in you again."

She nodded, then shrugged. "No. You lie back and let me get on you."

Spur laughed as Lila pushed him onto his back, then straddled his hips.

She positioned herself on top of him, then sank down, slowly impaling herself. She suddenly rocked back and forth, her face awash in ecstasy.

Spur stared up at her, watching her breasts move to the rhythm of her body as she worked herself to a frenzy. Lila's breath came in short, harsh gasps and she shuddered as a climax ripped through her. Her rocking increased in tempo and Spur felt her urgency, her need for him to push farther inside her. She brought herself to another climax but wouldn't stop.

Spur grabbed her buttocks and, lifting her gently, gave himself enough room to thrust up into her. She moaned as he drove harder and harder.

"Oh yes!" Lila cried. "Ride me, Spur. Ride me!"

With a grunt Spur sat up, grabbed Lila's waist, gently lifted her and then laid her down on her back. Lila raised her legs until her feet rested on Spur's hips, then sighed as he pounded into her.

"Harder," she said. "Harder and faster, Spur. Make me feel it all the way inside me!"

Driving furiously into her, Spur felt his own control break. She shivered, her eyes closed and her lips parted, as he rammed savagely into her, his hips thrusting uncontrollably, until his climax subsided.

He lay spend on top of her, knowing he was crushing her but unable to move, drained, exhausted. Lila's arms were still wrapped around his torso and her face was pressed against his sweaty chest. Her breath shot out in a warm stream across his right nipple.

She stirred after several minutes and he moved off her. Lila gently stroked his chest as they stared at each other in the still room.

"Lila?" Spur asked.

"Hmmmm?"

"Did you lose that last game of blackjack to me on purpose?"

She shook her head. "No, I didn't lose." She smiled deliciously. "I won."

EIGHT

By the time Spur had dressed and left Lila's room it was fully dark. He went to Wyler's Hotel and met Julie at the door as he walked in.

"Oh!" she said. "You scared me."

"Going somewhere? I could use a good supper."

"I'm just going out for a few minutes. I'll have some food for you in a half hour or so. How's that?"

"Fine. I'm going up to my room. I'll see you in the kitchen later."

"Right. I won't be gone long." She paused, as if she had something to say, then smiled and went out the door.

Spur climbed the stairs and went down the corridor. He stopped before his door and looked at the floor. The splinter he'd placed there was gone.

Someone had been in his room.

Julie? He didn't think so. She didn't seem the type. He remembered the raider who'd shot at him; maybe he had slipped inside Spur's room and stood there waiting even now.

Spur gently turned the knob and pushed the door inward a quarter of an inch, then darted back, bent to remove his boot, and flung it at the door with all the force he could muster.

It cracked loudly against the wood. The door swung open and a blinding explosion slammed Spur back against the hall wall. The building shook and then quieted; the sound of the blast faded.

The wind knocked from him, Spur stepped from the wall and peered into his room.

The light was bad but he could see that the room's contents had been destroyed. In the heaps of rubble within he couldn't see how the explosion had been set, but he could deduce that someone had rigged a shotgun to the door with a cord. When the door opened the shotgun fired into some sticks of dynamite, causing the explosion.

It had done its work. The door was nearly demolished, the walls shredded, the furniture sticks of wood. The sharp scent of dynamite stung his nostrils as he withdrew his head from the wrecked room. He retrieved his boot, which had managed to escape with minor scrapes, and pulled it on.

A door opened down the hall. "What the fuck's going on?" a brown-haired young man said, pulling up his pants.

"Nothing," Spur said. "Someone just set some dynamite to blow me up."

The man shook his head and closed his door.

The dynamite cleared up any questions he might have had; the raiders knew he was there to clean them up, and they weren't going to let him do it without a fight.

How they knew was a puzzle, and one that bothered Spur, but that would have to wait. Perhaps they didn't know for certain that Spur was on their trail, but they were making sure he didn't have the chance to do them any damage. It was logical. Rontrell was being careful.

Spur went to his bed and picked up his trusty Winchester from its hiding place beneath the mattress. The man must not have looked for it. He slung it over his shoulder and left the room, then took the stairs to the lobby.

Julie wasn't in sight, or in the kitchen, so he'd have to explain the blasted-out room later. He strode outside. It was dark. He had to find the man who was trying to kill him.

All he had to work with was the man's mount, the white horse with the small brown spots. He couldn't identify the man on sight, for he had worn a mask. Maybe the horse would give him the clue.

Spur traveled the length of Main Street twice, casually glancing at each horse standing quietly before the saloons and boarding houses. He must have looked at fifty horses on his first trip, and twice that after he'd shifted to the other side of Fargo's broad muddy Main Street, but the horse wasn't there. To make sure he hadn't somehow missed the animal in the darkness, he covered the same territory again, without success.

Spur leaned against a post and looked up at the stars; the moon hadn't risen yet and the night was still dark. The raider might have ridden out after setting the dynamite, or hidden his horse; it could be in a stable or tied up at the rail in front of some innocuous house somewhere else in Fargo.

Though Fargo wasn't a new town, it had grown

tenfold since the train had pushed through, and Spur didn't relish the thought of checking every horse in sight. If it did come to that, he'd ride the bay he'd hired at the livery stable; that was one job he wouldn't do on his feet.

Frustrated, Spur took out the bag of fixings he kept in his skirtpocket and rolled a smoke. He tore off a match, lit it, held it to the tip of the cigarette and inhaled deeply, watching a rider leave town.

As he was standing at the edge of Fargo, he quickly realized he had the advantage of seeing everyone who left town—at least those men who used this road, and who were going east.

Spur smoked and watched five men individually take the same road out. They left in five to ten minute intervals, and Spur maintained his position until he saw the first man ride back to town. Craning his neck, Spur saw him tie his horse to the hitching rail in front of a saloon.

Moments later another man, whom he recognized as one of those who'd just left, also came back into Fargo. The other three returned shortly.

Something was up, Spur thought. It smelled of trouble and he was itching to find out what it was. He went to Kelly's where he'd tied his horse, and mounted her, then rode east. The night was dark but the horse had no trouble following the trail that had been picked out among the two-foot-high scrub covering the area.

Ahead on the trail only solitary trees and an occasional small rise broke the monotony of the landscape. Looking over the area through the dim light, Spur saw that there were larger stands of trees in some areas, probably near rivers or streams, but the land was largely flat and featureless.

Away from the lights of Fargo, on a cloudy night, a man could get lost and roam for hours out there, Spur thought. Fortunately he had the stars to guide him, and the moon was rising.

Spur realized after ten minutes that there simply wasn't anything to see; whatever those men had left town for was evidently gone, or he'd missed it.

He pulled up the reins and the horse halted, but Spur's eyes caught something moving in the distance. It was dark but it almost looked like a man moving near a tree. He started the horse up again and presently stopped before the object.

It was a piece of red cloth that had been tied to a low-hanging branch of the old oak. The tree sat directly next to the trail, so it would have been easy for anyone to stop and tie it on. But for what reason?

He shook his head and turned his mount toward Fargo. It could be a message of some kind, but it was Greek to him. Spur rode back into Fargo without meeting anyone, as the moon slowly rose behind him in the east, illuminating the still night.

A raider—possibly all of the raiders—was after him. He couldn't stay at Julie's any more, at least not in the same room. He'd have to be ready to fight at every waking moment.

He smiled over these thoughts as the horse walked along the trail, with the lights of Fargo growing brighter every minute. By the time he'd reached the outskirts, he knew he could no longer enjoy the freedom he'd had in Fargo; he'd have to work primarily at night. He had known that it would come to this, but wished it hadn't happened so soon.

Restriction of his movements meant restriction of his ability to gather information on the raiders. He'd have to question people in private, if at all; move cautiously, and trust no one. His assignment, already tough, had grown more difficult.

Spur tied the bay up to the rail and went into Kelly's. The bar was crowded but he found elbow room and ordered a whiskey. He downed it quickly and asked for another. After he had finished the second shot Spur turned to look at a man who'd been staring at him while he was drinking.

The man averted his eyes; Spur glanced away from him and set down the glass.

Spur had seen the man for only a moment, but he'd burned the man's features into his brain. Perhaps it was nothing, but Spur wasn't willing to take any chances, now that he knew the raiders wanted him dead.

NINE

It was dark outside when Jake Castle left his small, lonely house in Fargo and swung up into his saddle. He rode slowly through town, listening to the laughter and music echoing out from the saloons, but rode past them. He had to be alone. He let the horse go where it wished, riding without destination. There were too many memories in Fargo—memories he'd have to erase if he expected to retain his sanity.

They were always worse at night, when things quieted down and he was alone at home. At work he didn't think about her more than once or twice a day.

Jake patted his horse's neck, moving gently back and forth in the saddle. God, how he needed a woman! It had been four months since Maggie died—four months of pure hell, four months without a woman.

Jake was surprised by the flow of blood he felt rushing to his groin; desire stirred within him. Against his will he remembered his last time with

73

Maggie, how he'd ridden her all night until they'd both collapsed in exhausted sleep.

Then, in the morning, he'd wakened with the sun in his eyes and Maggie stroking him into a frenzy. It had been their best night together.

A week later she was dead, of some sickness not even Doc Thomas could name. It wasn't fair, Jake told himself. It wasn't fair!

"Shit." His horse turned her head slightly, ears pricked up. "No, not you," Jake said, and rubbed her head.

As he rode, Jake thought of the blade he kept in his boot. It would be easy for him to slip it out, say his last prayer, and then plunge it deep into his chest, ending his misery forever. Yes, it would be quick and clean, a farewell to a life that had been nothing but misery. He could do it without thinking twice.

But he didn't. Jake felt a rage build inside him; a rage against everything in creation. Something had taken his wife from him.

He transformed his sorrow into anger and within moments was sitting straighter in the saddle and feeling his fury. He wouldn't take the coward's way out. He'd grab life by the balls and take it for everything it had.

Hell, why should he work? It was boring. He could steal what he needed or wanted, living in a town for a while until someone caught wise and wanted to string him up, then moving on.

Jake laughed, pulled a cheroot from his shirt pocket and lit up. He had enjoyed the smoke for a good three minutes when he felt the need to empty his bladder. He let the horse wander off the trail, tied it to a young sapling, and walked up to a bush a few yards away. He had stuck his cheroot between his teeth and reached for his fly, when he heard something move in the darkness.

He paused and searched the ground around him; he could see nothing, just a clump of trees several yards away where the land seemed to drop down a bit. Jake shrugged, unbuttoned his britches and had just gotten it out when he felt a muzzle press against his spine.

"Don't move," a voice said in his ear.

"I won't," Jake said, spitting the cheroot from his mouth. "What do you want? I ain't got no money with me. You can have my gun, but that's all I got."

"We don't want your gun."

Jake was more angry than scared at the intrusion. Why the hell did he have to get bushwhacked just when he was feeling good again?

A hand gently pulled his Colt from his holster, then he felt the muzzle move away from his spine.

"All right, boy; turn around nice and slow so I can get a look at you."

Jake did as he was told and stared at the masked man curiously. What did he want? The man looked at Jake and burst out laughing.

"Holy shit, boy. What were you doing, playing with yourself?"

"What?"

Between guffaws the masked man waved the barrel of his Colt at Jake's crotch.

He shrugged and stuffed himself back in, then buttoned his pants. "I was going to take a piss. Who are you? What do you want?"

"Never mind that now. Just come with me."

He motioned for Jake to move ahead of him and they walked through the underbrush toward the stand of trees. The gunman pushed Jake harshly. He lost his footing and rolled down a steep embankment, tasting dirt, and finally landed in a painful heap twenty feet below the cliff.

His captor laughed as Jake rose to his feet. It was then that he saw the fire and the men gathered around it. Most stood looking at him, and all wore masks.

"We've got a new man, Mr. Rontrell."

One of the company who had been squatting near the fire rose to his full height and quickly adjusted his mask, an almost unconscious gesture to ensure that he could not be recognized by the stranger.

"Found him on my watch," Jake's captor said. "He was nosing around up there. Thought I'd bring him in. It looked like that Spur character until I turned him around."

The tall man approached Jake. "Jake Castle, isn't it?" he said in a gruff voice.

"Yes. What is this, anyway? I was taking a piss and I get a gun at my back. Is it against the law or something?"

"No; we have to be careful." He moved closer to Jake. "Don't you know who we are?"

Jake started to shake his head, but remembered that night in town when the general store had been hit.

"Are you the raiders?"

"Very good. And I'm Rontrell."

Jake looked at the six men gathered around the fire. But there had been more raiders than that. Hell, he'd seen more than that in town on one raid.

"You're wondering about our number? We're not all here tonight, just the leaders. We've got a good organization, Jake. And after tonight you'll be one of us."

"I don't want to be one of you."

"The alternative is death."

Jake was silent, but his anger flared. He was trapped; he had to join the raiders. But wasn't that a blessing? Wouldn't that be an outlet for his hostility? He could stay right there in Fargo and wage his battle against mankind, to soothe the wound that Maggie's death had opened.

Rontrell was looking at him. "If you're thinking you wouldn't tell anything to anyone about our meeting tonight, you're wrong. You would. And to ensure that never happens, you'll become one of us." Rontrell stepped back and the men rose.

"How're you gonna do that? Some kind of ceremony or something? It don't matter to me; I've decided to join up. Hell, maybe that's what I need."

"Smart man, Castle. Damn smart." Rontrell extended his hand.

Jake took a step forward and reached to grasp it when Rontrell swiftly raised his left and smashed it against Jake's head. He staggered back from the blow, then looked at Rontrell furiously.

"You son of a bitch!"

"Just a test. To be a raider," Rontrell said in an even but gruff voice, "you must always be on your guard. You men are much too valuable to get your-

77

selves killed. You are always to be on the defensive; if anyone so much as hints around that he thinks you are a raider, you must kill him without hesitation. This is our only regulation, apart from following my orders. Do you understand, Mr. Castle?"

He rubbed his head and nodded.

"Good. Then you'll be party to all our activities from now on. You'll be know as 'Y.' Remember that; no one will call you by your real name, and the rest of the men—those not present tonight—won't even know your real name. Answer to 'Y' and you'll do just fine. In time you'll know every man's code letter."

"Right," Jake said.

"Not far from here on the trail is an old oak tree. That's where we hang our signals; if there's a red rag hanging from one of the branches, that means there's a meeting, but only for the leaders—you won't have to attend. If there's a blue rag, that's an open meeting; you have to be here. Meeting times are usually eight P.M. unless we're working on a raid. Stop by the tree and look to see if there's a meeting, if no one's told you. Understand?"

"Sure."

"Good. That's about it. You can join us for the rest of the meeting, so sit yourself down by the fire and we'll get back to business."

Jake moved closer to the blaze and found a spot to sit. The others followed and Rontrell began outlining their next raid; it was to be a small but important one and it wouldn't happen for at least a week, maybe longer. They wanted to lay low while

Spur McCoy was in town.

" 'J' nearly killed Spur today," Rontrell said. "Twice. Once out in the back country, and then at his hotel. Both times he failed. Hell, I didn't even want him to try the second time, but I couldn't get word to him. I don't know where 'J' is, and frankly I don't care. I think he's been informed by now to stop trying to kill Spur.

"Watch Spur, but don't touch him. I don't want Spur to be killed and start a big ruckus. If he gets too close, do what you have to do. Just don't do anything before then; lay low and let him play his games. Hopefully he'll leave and we won't have to think about him again. Is that clear?"

The men grunted their answers, and Rontrell seemed to accept them.

"That's all for tonight. We'll meet again next Friday, if I don't call another meeting before that. Pass the word."

The men rose and, in silence, went to their respective mounts and left the area. Jake stumbled up the hill, found his horse and rode from the area as quickly as he could.

For a moment while Rontrell had been talking Jake was sure he recognized him, but then discounted the idea; the voice was too low, too harsh. He couldn't remember anyone in town sounding like that, though he supposed it could be an altered voice.

Jake rode hard back to Fargo, glad that the night was so light. Had he done the right thing in joining the raiders? Actually he hadn't been given a choice, so it was all for the better.

He couldn't believe that not long ago he'd thought about killing himself. Now that wasn't good enough. He wanted to live and get something out of life—something for himself, something he could be proud of.

Jake felt his erection grow again. He smiled and decided he'd have a roll with one of the saloon girls. Hell, why not? He'd let his anger and grief hold him back long enough.

It was time to start living.

TEN

Spur left Kelly's Saloon and returned to his hotel, where he met Julie on the walk outside the door.

"Hello," she said.

"Have you been back to the hotel since the last time I saw you?"

"Yes. I told you I wouldn't be gone long."

"Then you know about the dynamite?"

"The what? Oh, that explosion upstairs. Yes, but I didn't know it was done with dynamite."

"It was. Someone tried to kill me."

"Are you sure?" Julie asked, her face halfway to suspicion.

"Why else would someone set dynamite to go off in my room?"

"Fortunately they didn't succeed. You weren't hurt either, were you?"

"No. But only because I was careful."

"I see. Let's go in. I'll get you another room."

"Thanks."

They entered the hotel and Julie went straight to the front desk to look at the register.

"I've had a lot of business since the Drake and Mason burned up. Thirteen and twenty-four are open."

"Are either of them at the end of the building facing the street?"

"Twenty-four is."

"I'll take it." He reached into his pocket, pulled out some money and laid it on the counter before her. "Take this."

"Why?"

"For the damage upstairs."

"That wasn't your fault." She shook her head and smiled.

"But it wouldn't have happened if I hadn't checked in here."

"True." She touched the money, then picked it up and stuffed it into her purse. "Only since you're insisting."

"Thanks." He handed her the key to his old room and she exchanged it for the new.

"Turn left at the top of the stairs and go all the way to the end of the hall."

"I almost hesitate to take another room here; I don't want that blown up too."

"You have to stay somewhere, Spur; it might as well be here."

"Thanks again."

He left the front desk, climbed the stairs, and went to his old room. If he were right he'd left his carpetbag beneath the bed. Had it been destroyed by the blast?

He peered into the darkness, with only two pools of moonlight streaming in through the shattered windows to guide his eyes. Yes, he saw a patch of color under the collapsed bed. Spur stepped over a pile of charred timbers and went to it. He gripped the handle and returned to the hall, then went down it until he came to Number 24. Spur pushed the key into the hole, turned it and opened the door.

He lit the kerosene lamp, lowered the flame gently, and looked around. The room was identical to his last, even to the color of the blankets and the design on the basin and pitcher. Spur paused to remove the rifle from his back, leaned it against the bed, and went to the window.

He had a clear view of the street, as he had hoped. Spur looked down to see his rented bay standing peacefully where he'd tied her up.

He then glanced down Main Street; it was quiet. Few men moved along the broad, dusty expanse, and no women. The raiders must be responsible for that, he thought grimly. He saw another horse and sighed, thinking of the spotted one the man who'd been trying to shoot him had been riding. It must be somewhere in town.

He casually inspected each horse in his field of vision; the moonlight wasn't bright enough for positive identification, but Spur did it anyway to pass the time.

Then, tied up in front of a boarding house, he saw a white horse with tiny brown spots.

It could be the same one, but he wouldn't know until he went outside and got a closer look. Spur slung his Winchester over his back, turned the lamp flame down low and left his room, making sure to lock it firmly before he went to the stairs and then outside.

He walked swiftly across the street and approached the boarding house. It wasn't until he was almost there that he realized, with a start, that the spotted horse was gone.

Spur checked every animal tied up at the rail, but the one he wanted to see had vanished. An empty space at the rail marked where the horse had been before it was moved.

Spur cursed under his breath, shook his head and returned to his room, where he kept the lamp down, moved a chair to the window, and sat, watching the spot where he'd seen the animal, until weariness overtook him and he fell into a deep sleep, slumped down in his chair, his head thrown back across the chair's top rung.

Sunlight stabbed at his eyelids, forcing Spur to waken as the day began. His body ached from sleeping in the chair, but he quickly remembered why he was sitting as he was and glanced down to Main Street.

Tied to the hitching rail was the spotted horse.

At his first glance, now that the horse was fully illuminated, he was sure it was the same one the raider had ridden. He had to keep an eye on it and wait for its owner to return. Spur felt his stomach growl; he hadn't eaten yet. But that would have to wait. He had to watch the horse.

Twenty minutes later Spur heard a knock on the door.

"Yes?" he said, not looking away from the horse.

"Can I come in?" Julie's voice.

"Sure."

She entered the room and looked at him. "I was wondering if I should save some breakfast for you."

"That sounds good, but do you think you could bring it up here? I can't leave right now."

"Not even for a minute?" Julie asked curiously.

"No. I'd appreciate it if you could bring it up."

She sighed. "All right. But if you're going to be wanting this regularly, it'll cost you extra."

"I'll pay it; don't worry," Spur said, in a mutter, still watching the animal.

She laughed. "I was joking, Spur. I'll bring it right up."

She left.

The horse hadn't been moved when Julie opened Spur's door and the sharp scent of freshly cooked bacon and rich coffee filled the air.

"As you wished, breakfast in your room. Where should I put this?"

Spur finally turned from the window. "What?"

She frowned, holding the tray in front of her. "Where do you want me to set this down?"

"Oh, right there," he said, pointing to the small writing table next to the window. "That'll be fine."

Julie nodded and placed the tray on the table. "I've got twelve more hungry men to feed, so I can't stay and chat. Not that you seem in a talkative mood anyway. Enjoy your breakfast. Don't worry about the dishes; I'll come up and get them later."

"Fine. And thanks for the service, Julie."

"No problem." She turned and exited.

Spur ate with relish, occasionally looking away

from the window, and was soon finished. He left the dishes on the table and turned back to watch the horse.

He grew impatient, wondering why its owner hadn't claimed it yet. And he wondered where it had been taken last night when he'd gone out to check whether it was the same horse or not.

He shook his head. Spur stood, took a last glance at the horse, then ran out of his room, down the hall and stairs, and out the front door.

The horse was still there. He approached it, glancing around him, and saw no one. The animal snorted softly as Spur circled it, checking it out. Yes, it was the same horse—he was sure. He'd watch it until someone claimed it.

Wearily Spur returned to his hotel room, took his seat by the window, and watched the horse. It would be a long day.

Just at dusk Spur yawned and stretched. His impatience had changed to a vague wish that something, anything, would happen to break the monotony.

He raised a glass of whiskey to his lips and took a sip, then put it down. Maybe when it grew dark someone would claim the horse. Someone—the raider—might know he was watching.

He rejected the idea and had another sip of the whiskey. No, he was letting his imagination get the best of him. Spur sighed and stared dully at the horse.

At least Julie would bring more food soon; that would give him something to do. Spur finished his glass of whiskey and picked up the bottle, but decided against drinking. He didn't want the alcohol to get in the way of his concentration. Spur prepared himself for spending the night at the window watching the horse; he couldn't fall asleep until he saw the raider again.

Spur sighed, stretched out his feet and laid his head on the back of the chair, padded by his hands. It was as comfortable a position as he had found.

Seconds later the window shattered, sending shards of glass flying into Spur's room. He immediately covered his face; as he listened to the glass raining down on the floor from two more rounds that blasted into the wall behind him.

Someone was firing at his window. Why? When it was safe, he uncovered his face and straightened up from the chair, then ducked as another round ripped into the room.

He remembered the horse. Spur lifted his head and peered out the window to the rail. The horse was gone, but dust filled the street. Whoever had shot out his window had taken the horse and fled.

ELEVEN

Spur dusted bits of glass from his clothing and, after slinging his rifle onto his back, went to the street where the horse had been. The raider who owned it had known Spur was watching him and had been careful. Spur knew the horse wouldn't show in town again, not as long as he was there. The raiders would be too careful for that.

A sour feeling in his gut, Spur turned, saw Kelly's Saloon, and headed for it. He might as well have a drink, as long as he didn't have a horse to watch.

Spur entered the saloon and saw Lila standing at the piano, plunking out a simple tune, singing to herself. Spur approached her and saw the enraptured expression on her face. Lila was oblivious to the noise and the people around her.

She opened her eyes and looked at him.

"I lost a horse," he said.

"Sorry. I don't know that one." Her eyes sparkled.

"Ever think about singing for a living?" His mood lightened. "You're good enough to get paid for it."

"Thanks, Spur. I've thought about it, but never had the urge. I guess I'm happy with what I'm doing."

"Playing poker and sweeping up?"

"Hey, you trying to run my life or something?" She was smiling.

"No. Just feeling ornery."

"Anyway, I don't see how I could support myself singing. Oh maybe in Denver or St. Louis. But here in Fargo? No. People would rather play cards than listen to a girl sing."

"Just a suggestion," Spur said, and then glanced at the bar.

"You look like you need a drink. I'll get one for you; why don't you find us a table in the back?" She moved gracefully toward the bar, her hips gently swaying.

Spur selected a table not far from the piano. No one was near enough to listen to them, which was exactly what Spur wanted.

Lila returned with the drinks and sat down. They sipped.

"You know a man in town with a snow-white horse covered with brown spots no bigger than a thumbnail?"

"Why?"

"Just wondering."

"I see. Well, none comes to mind, but then I don't spend most of my time staring at horses."

"Are you sure? I'd like to know, if you do know the man."

"No. Sorry. Like I said, I don't make it a habit to memorize every man's mount. Why? You in some kind of trouble?"

"No. Just wondering."

Lila gave him a wink and tapped her fingernails on the table.

"All right, Spur. I can take a hint. You don't want to talk about it."

"That's right."

"Fine. So what do we talk about? I would mention the fact that someone just tried to blow you up at your hotel room, but I don't suppose you'd comment on that, either."

Spur looked at her in silence.

"Or the fact that someone unloaded a few rounds into your window not more than ten minutes ago."

"How do you know all this?"

She spread her hands. "Fargo's a small town. Word travels fast. Besides, we all heard the rifle shots. Some guy said he saw a man ride away on a spotted horse."

"So?"

She frowned. "Spur McCoy, you're the most frustrating man I've ever met!"

"Thanks. I appreciate that."

"All right, don't tell me. I guess you have your reasons. But if you ever need any help, don't think twice about asking. I'm a pushover for a guy in trouble." She looked at Spur, then quickly away. "Hey, you want to come to my place tonight?" she asked. "I'm off work now and I hate to go home alone."

"You're shameless, Lila. You know that? Absolutely shameless."

"That's right. But I just remembered I can't take you home—not yet. The town meeting. I should go." She snapped her fingers in mock dismay.

91

"What meeting?"

"Zane—he's our mayor—he's decided to call a meeting to talk about these raiders who've been pestering us." She looked at Spur and smiled. "You wouldn't be interested in coming along, would you?"

"I might be talked into it." He downed the contents of his glass and set it on the table. "When does it start?"

She glanced at the clock over the bar. "Ten minutes. Should we go?"

"Sure. It's a way to pass the evening."

They stood and left Kelly's.

Moments later Lila hustled Spur into the town hall.

"If you don't get here early you have to stand in the back. Fargo's growing fast but they've never built a new town hall." They sat near the back of the room.

Spur felt the tension in the air as conversations about the raiders erupted. Hints, rumors and dark retellings circulated around him.

"See that fat, balding man over there, leaning against the wall? That's Zane Evans, our mayor. And that tall gaunt one next to him is our sheriff, Mel McCormick. Mel and Zane don't get along well; I can't imagine why they're standing talking like that."

While they sat and Lila pointed out people to Spur, more than a hundred citizens of Fargo crowded into the building. At six-fifteen Zane Evans walked to the podium and called for silence.

"I'm not going to mince words here," he said in a

booming voice while fiddling with the gold watch chain that stretched across his ample belly. "We've got a big problem—Rontrell's Raiders—and a solution has to be found." The mayor coughed and continued. "If any of you have come here tonight thinking I have the solution, you're wrong. But that is precisely why I called this meeting—to find out what your ideas are and to see if between us we can map out a way to rid ourselves of Rontrell and his men."

The audience was silent as Zane pulled a handkerchief from his pants pocket and dabbed at his forehead. "At first it wasn't anything serious—window smashing and maybe a little cattle stampeding. But now these men have started killing people, and that's got to stop. First Buck; now Clyde Riley's dead not more than two days and the Drake and Mason hotel is burned to the ground, with Drake, Mason and his dear sweet wife, Esther, inside!"

"Let's string them all up!" a man from the crowd yelled.

"That's fine, but we have to know who they are before we can do that," the mayor said. "Any ideas?"

There were a few comments but no one stood and presented a rational plan.

"What about you, Sheriff? You got something that'll wipe out Rontrell?" the mayor asked.

Mel McCormick stood. "No. And frankly, I'm moving slow. Last time I tried anything Buck got killed." The thin man shook his head. "I'm not going to risk that. I can't risk it."

Lila leaned closer to Spur, touched his shoulder,

and whispered into his ear. "Buck was Mel's deputy. After a raid in town, Buck galloped off to follow the raiders. Next morning he was found all cut up and laid in pieces outside the sheriff's office."

Spur nodded and returned his attention to the mayor.

"I understand your position, Sheriff McCormick, but maybe Buck's was the only way."

"That's right!" A young man, his face infused with inspiration, stood. "The next time they pull a raid, let's all mount up and ride after them, just like Buck did. Sure, Buck's dead and I'm sorry about that, but maybe if some of us had gone along with him he'd be alive today and Rontrell would be either six feet under or in jail. That's the answer. If we ride out together, twenty or thirty of us, they wouldn't have a chance!"

"But the raids happen so fast," the sheriff said, still standing. "You never know when they're going to ride into town, and usually it's done with very few people around."

"Then whoever sees them will have to tell the others about them. We'll mount up and ride out after them!"

"By then it would be too late," the sheriff said.

"Strength in numbers!" the younger man said. "That's the answer! Strength in numbers!"

After a buzz from the crowd had died out, the mayor spoke.

"That seems to be the best plan so far. All right, now we have to address its problems. As the sheriff pointed out, few people are aware of a raid while it is taking place. We have to devise some sort of signal to let everyone in town know what's happening, to prepare. Any ideas on that point?''

One man stood and began to speak.

Spur sighed and folded his arms, listening, realizing how desperate the people of Fargo were.

Nearly an hour later the mayor called a halt to the meeting. The suggestion had been discussed and measures had been worked out for people to alert each other of a raid in progress.

Lila and Spur left the hall and walked out into the night. Clouds scuttled across the moon.

"What about the mayor, Zane Evans?" Spur asked.

"What about him?"

"Is he the kind of man you can trust?"

Lila laughed. "He's got fast hands, but I think I could trust him. Why?"

"Just wondering. I'd like to get some information from him."

"Here's your chance. He's just leaving."

Spur turned and saw the mayor walk briskly from the town hall and turn abruptly to his right.

"He's probably on his way to his office," Lila said.

"Where's that?"

"Right there." She pointed to a small squat white structure half a block away.

"Thanks."

"Will I see you later tonight?"

"Maybe. I don't know what I'll be doing yet."

She took his hand. "I'll be upset if you don't show up at my room."

"Don't count on it—not tonight at least. I have to

95

catch the mayor."

She pouted, then shrugged. "Okay. See you later, Spur. And I sincerely hope so."

Spur smiled and hurried down the street toward the mayor. He reached the man just as he was standing before the door to his office.

"Mayor Evans?" Spur said.

"Yes. Can I help you?" The mayor looked at him curiously.

"I hope so. Can we go in?"

"What? Oh, yes."

At that moment the door to the office opened and a pale, tired-eyed man stepped out.

"Frazer, where do you think you're going?" the mayor said.

"Nowhere. Just out to get a quick drink. Come on, Zane; I've been working all day and all night. Can't I get one drink before I go back to work?"

His words were lost in the roar of several rapidly approaching horses. Spur thought nothing of it until he remembered the raiders. He turned and saw the men charging directly at him. There wasn't time to look at their number or to get any details of the horses, he grabbed the mayor and pushed him inside the room, then shut the door behind them.

Spur stood, his Colt drawn, waiting for the door to open.

TWELVE

"What the hell you doing?" the mayor asked, angry.

"Those were the raiders, or hadn't you noticed?" Spur said as he stood with his Colt drawn inside the mayor's office.

"How do you know that?"

The sharp sound of a gun firing answered the question. Another rang out, and Spur instinctively backed from the door. He knelt behind the desk that stood in the center of the room. The mayor wisely followed suit. Moments later the door burst open and a man stormed in, his Colt firing wildly.

Spur killed him with a chest shot. He fired again but quickly had no targets; the men who had stood behind the first quickly disappeared, and Spur heard the sounds of hooves beating the ground. He stood cautiously, decided that the downed man was dead, and jumped over his body into the night air outside the mayor's office.

The last of the raiders rounded a corner and was lost to his eyes.

Spur looked around, found a horse, jumped onto it and spurred it into a full run, following the raiders. He hoped the mayor would have the good sense to make sure the raider he'd shot was either dead or talking.

Spur moved around the corner and saw them a thousand feet ahead of him. The mount was questioning his commands, holding back, but Spur got the feel of the animal and it began cooperating with him. It was a sleek, sturdy, fast horse and Spur soon halved the distance between himself and the raiders.

A few of the men fired over their shoulders, but none came close to threatening him. He pushed his horse faster and gained more ground, then drew his Colt.

He peeled off a shot and missed, tried another and struck home with one of the slowest raiders. The man screamed and fell from his horse, rolled twice, and came to a halt.

Spur fired again but the remaining raiders moved faster away from him. They were out of his reach, and since he didn't know their destination he couldn't hope to cut across country to save time. So he trotted back to the prone man he'd shot, tied up his horse, and approached him.

The raider lay, his face twisted with agony beneath the mask, holding his side. His weapon was five feet from him, forgotten. Spur bent, took the gun, tucked it under his belt and went over.

"Who are you?" he asked, looking at the man in the darkness.

For the first time the raider realized he wasn't alone. He reached for his holster, but Spur motioned to the weapon he'd taken, then bent and gripped the mask. With a savage motion he ripped it from the man's head.

The face meant nothing to him, but he was sure it would to someone in Fargo. Spur dragged the moaning, kicking man to a rock, sat him up and stood behind him.

"I should kill you," he said. "I should cut you open and let the sun fry your guts. But I can't, because you could be useful to me. First I want the names of all the other raiders."

"Go to hell," the man said.

"If you're no help to me, I will kill you. Sure as shit you're not worth saving."

"I won't tell you anything," the man said between clenched teeth.

"I think you might change your mind."

"I ain't afraid of dying," he said, and pressed his hands against his wound.

"I figured that. But you might not want to keep on living after I'm through with you."

The man's eyes betrayed his fear, even in the darkness. Spur didn't want to damage permanently the man, nor did he want to wait too long for a doctor to look at that wound. Time was important; if the man didn't talk now, there might be no chance later.

Spur took a step closer to the man and folded his arms on his chest. "You going to talk?"

"Make me." The eyes glinted in the darkness.

Spur slammed his booted foot between the man's widespread legs. He howled and doubled up with the pain, his scream piercing the silent night, sending a bird fluttering nearby up to the clouds.

"Talk!" Spur said.

The man sputtered.

"What?"

"I can't tell you what I don't know."

Spur waited until the raider sat up before ramming his knee to the man's chin. This time the man didn't cry out, but the force of the impact sent his head and torso flying backward. Spur heard his back hit the dirt.

"Talk!"

"No." Quieter this time.

"Who are the other raiders?"

Spur knelt and grabbed the man's head. "Who are they?"

The eyes were nearly closed; blood flowed from a new cut on the chin, and the man's shirt was soaked from the bullet wound.

"I don't know." The raider swallowed loudly. "They don't tell us each other's name. Only numbers or letters."

"Who's your leader?"

"I don't know!" he said, with more force. "All I know is that one new guy joined—Jake Castle. He's the only one I know about. That's 'cause he stumbled onto us one night and Rontrell said his name out loud."

This made sense to Spur; if the men didn't identify each other, they couldn't incriminate themselves. He nodded and looked up; the man's horse stood nearby.

"All right. We're going to town. Can you sit on your horse?"

The man nodded weakly. Spur helped him to his feet as the man moaned loudly, then got him onto the horse. Spur found two lengths of rope on his borrowed mount and used the first to bind the man's hands behind him, then tied the other to the horse to serve as a lead.

Spur mounted and led the horse and rider with him toward Fargo. Fortunately he could see the lights of the town; otherwise he might have some trouble finding it in the darkness with nothing but the stars to guide him.

Spur thought over the man's words, watching him gently sway in the saddle as they rode. Twice he thought the man would all from his horse but both times he recovered his balance.

"Can you talk now?" Spur asked.

The man grunted an affirmative response.

"What's your name?"

"Charlie Vendrick."

"How long have you been a raider?"

"Shit, I don't know."

"Try."

"Two months, I'd guess."

"What's your purpose? What is Rontrell trying to accomplish with these raids?"

"Damned if I know. Most of us guys went along with it for the fun—and the money. Shit, this town was too tame. None of us cared why Rontrell had us do what he did; we just went along with him."

Spur nodded. The man wasn't going to be much help. But he did have a name to work with—Jake Castle. He couldn't wait to get back to town and start digging for some answers.

Without warning Spur heard the sharp report of a rifle. Charlie Vendrick slumped over on his horse, then slid off.

Spur urged his horse to a gallop as rounds whispered past him, finally slowing when he realized he wasn't being followed.

The raiders must have decided not to let one of their own reveal their secrets, so they had set up the ambush to kill him and, Spur thought, probably himself as well. He wondered why they had let him go, but decided he couldn't be too important to them. Their main objective was to kill their own man so he couldn't betray them.

Spur wearily rode into town and tied the horse where he'd found it. When he located the owner he'd apologize and thank him for the use of the horse.

Spur had walked ten feet from the rail when he saw the sheriff rapidly approaching him. He was glad; he had a few things to tell the man.

"Mr. McCoy?" McCormick said as he met Spur.

"That's right."

The sheriff drew his gun. "You'll have to come with me."

"I don't understand," Spur said. "I just followed the raiders. I captured one of them and got some information from him, but they killed him before I could bring him back here."

"Good story, but you'll have to do better than that, McCoy. Come with me and there won't be any trouble."

Spur shook his head. "You don't seem to understand."

McComrick motioned with his weapon, a grim, determined but slightly angry look on his face. "You're under arrest, Rontrell."

102

THIRTEEN

Spur stared at Sheriff McCormick incredulously. "What?"

"You're under arrest. Turn around and walk."

"Why?"

"For starters," the man said, never lowering his gun, "you stole Ned's horse."

"I borrowed it," Spur said.

"That's for the judge to decide. And that's only half of it. Seems the mayor's sure your name is Rontrell."

"I don't believe it," Spur said.

"Get moving. We can talk about this later."

Spur glanced at the weapon, shook his head, and walked toward the sheriff's office. It made less sense the more he thought about it. How could the mayor—or anyone else, for that matter—think he was Rontrell?

Once at the jail, McCormick opened the door and pushed Spur inside the room. Spur turned to his right and saw a gaunt but potbellied man of twenty-three sitting behind a desk snoozing, his feet propped up. When the door banged shut the younger man shot to his feet.

"Who? What?" he said, looking wildly around.

"Just me, Herman. I've got a prisoner. The mayor's sure this man's Rontrell. Hand me the keys to the cell."

The taller man, his left eye twitching nervously, took the keyring from a drawer in the desk and handed it to the sheriff.

"Here you are. So this is Rontrell, eh? I don't remember having seen him around much before the last few days. Are you sure the mayor's right about this?"

"You've never seen Rontrell's face; no one has except the raiders. So there's no way of knowing for sure—yet."

Herman shrugged. "Okay. Just wondering."

Spur stood watching as the sheriff unlocked the small cell at the back of the building, then stepped inside when the man motioned him to do so. The sheriff closed the door.

"There's nothing I can do now—not with the mayor so sure about this."

"What's he been telling you?" Spur asked, standing, looking at the sheriff between the steel-blue bars.

"Zane's got it all worked out in his head. He says you've been leading the raiders for some time but you haven't been living in Fargo. He says that's why no one's been able to identify you. He thinks you were holed up on a ranch not far from here. Now you've moved in and are directing things up close. And now that the raiders have started killing people, he says we should have you behind bars to put an end to the raiding."

"Did the mayor explain why, if I were Rontrell and were leading the raids from outside of town, I'd risk everything and start showing my face in Fargo?"

"I had the same thought," McCormick said, sitting behind the desk. "He says you're trying to throw us off guard; if we saw you here we'd assume you were another visitor from out of town, and not think twice about you. But the mayor says you've been sneaking around Fargo asking questions. And you've been nearby during the last few raids as well."

"So that makes me Rontrell?" Spur said, anger slashing through his voice. "It's horseshit!"

"About your being Rontrell? Probably. But you did steal Ned's horse."

"Right after the raid at the mayor's office I ran outside. I saw the raiders riding away, so I grabbed the nearest horse and followed. I managed to wound one man and question him. His name was Charlie Vendrick."

The sheriff looked up. "Vendrick a raider? Impossible. He's a good friend of mine. Known him for years."

"He said he knew only one other raider by name—Jake Castle. I was taking Vendrick back here to Fargo when we were ambushed—and Vendrick was killed. I barely got back to town alive. If you don't believe me, check up on Vendrick. See if he's around town. You won't find him."

"Where exactly did all this take place?" the

sheriff asked.

"West. A mile out of town; maybe more. I can take you there."

"Sorry. Not yet. But I'll check into your story." The sheriff turned his back on Spur and lit a cigar.

The agent cursed under his breath and sat on the stinking cot that was pushed against the cell's back wall. With one small barred window above him and the steel bars locked before him, Spur didn't have a chance to escape. He'd have to wait out the time.

But as he sat and wondered at the mayor's accusation, Spur couldn't help but suspect the mayor of deliberately lying to get Spur in jail.

Why?

An hour later McCormick left, probably to go to sleep, and Herman was left in charge. Spur recognized the kind of kid he was; full of enthusiasm and aggression, and likely to get himself killed at the first opportunity. Spur listened to Herman's rumblings but was busy with his own thoughts.

"Yeah, McCormick picked me as his deputy because I was the best qualified of anyone in town. Not that there were many who wanted the job, I'll admit." He lit up a cheroot. "But I did, so he gave it to me. My friends said I was crazy, especially after Buck had just been killed by you raiders. But I wasn't afraid of you. I ain't afraid of no one."

"I've told you—I'm not Rontrell. I'm not a raider."

"So you say. You're just trying to save our own ass from the noose, Rontrell. Hell, I knew there was something wrong with you the day you came into

Fargo. I even mentioned it to McCormick, but he ignored me. If only he'd looked into you then, maybe the last few raids wouldn't have happened."

"I had nothing to do with them."

"Says you."

"Why's the mayor so sure I'm Rontrell? Not more than a few hours ago I was with him behind his desk in his office getting shot at. He sure didn't seem to mind my saving his life then, by pulling him into his office as the raiders rode up."

Herman gaffawed, puffed, and spoke. "Shit, Zane was just playing along with you. He knew you were crooked all the time."

Spur shook his head; it wasn't right. The mayor wouldn't do an about face that quickly unless there was pressure on him. But from whom? Why was it so important for the raiders to have him locked up? Were they afraid of him?

Spur turned to look at Herman; he'd dozed off with his cheroot still between his lips. As Spur watched, a length of ash fell from its tip onto the man's shirt.

He stretched out on the cot and tried to sleep, but the front door to the jail burst open and he heard a woman's voice calling his name.

"Spur? Spur, I don't believe this!" Lila said as she walked up to his cell.

"Just hold on," Herman said, awake now and standing next to his desk. "Where do you think you're going?"

"To see Spur," she said, her teeth clenched.

Herman shrugged and returned to his chair, then flashed a look at Lila. "I sure never thought you'd get mixed up with a fella like Rontrell, Lila."

She swung around.

"Spur is not Rontrell, you idiot!" She shook her head and walked to the cell.

"How are you, Spur?" She gave him a searching look.

"Fine." He rose from the cot and went to her. "But I wonder about the rest of the town."

"I can't imagine how this got started."

"Ask your mayor."

"I heard about that; it's not like him, Spur. It's just not like him."

"You know a man named Charlie Vendrick?" Spur lowered his voice as he spoke.

"Sure; why?"

"He's dead."

"What?"

"Just after I left you to talk with the mayor we were raided."

"I know; I heard about it. Zane's foolproof plan for alerting the city was a farce; no one knew about the raid until it was over."

"Someone didn't do his part, I guess. Anyway, I got a horse and rode after them, but only managed to shoot one man. He was wounded, not dead, so I questioned him; he said he was Charlie Vendrick and he only knew one other raider's name—Jack Castle."

"I know him too; he's lived here for years. Jake lost his wife early this year."

"Hey, what are you two talking about over there?" Herman asked from his desk.

"Nothing," Lila said.

"When I was bringing Vendrick back to town the

raiders ambushed us and killed him. Then when I'm back in Fargo I'm arrested. I told the sheriff what had happened, but he's not looking into it—as far as I know."

"That's McCormick," Lila said. "The only thing he hates more than the raiders are any leads about them. He's afraid of getting himself killed—like Buck did."

"I can't see what throwing me into jail is going to accomplish for the raiders."

"You think they're behind this?" Lila asked, her eyes wide. "But I thought you said Zane got you in here?"

"They could have forced him into it, or he could be one of them. Either way, they're responsible."

"Whatcha doing," Herman yelled from his chair, "whispering sweet nothings into each other's ears?"

"Yeah, and that's as close as you'll ever come to hearing them from me!" Lila snapped in mock rage.

"Check up on Jake and Vendrick, if you have the time, would you?" Spur asked.

"Sure. And get yourself out of here. I can't wait to be with you again."

She smiled, walked to the door and left without speaking to Herman.

The deputy stood and shook his head. "I never figured she'd go for a character like you, Rontrell." He smiled. "Hell, Lila could have any man in town. Fact is, she's had half of them, at least!"

Spur sat on his bunk and pulled his bag of fixings from his shirtpocket, then rolled a smoke. He tore off a match and lit it, puffed at the cigarette and thought.

A quiet cry startled Spur out of his sleep.

The first hint of dawn crept in through the barred window above his cot. He sat, blinked, and saw two men moving through the jail. One was busy tying the unconscious Herman to his chair, the other approached his cell.

"Spur, we've come to get you out of here."

"Who the hell are you?" He sat and yawned.

"Never mind that. We've been sent by friends of yours who want you out. We've got horses waiting outside."

The man was short, stocky, with full muttonchop sideburns and moustache. He held the key to the cell in his right hand. Friends of his? He had no friends in Fargo, save for Lila and Julie; but neither of them would plan something like this.

He shook his head; this didn't sound good.

Just as the man fit the key into the lock Spur saw the front door open. Mel McCormick summed up the situation, drew and fired once, then slammed the door shut in front of him. The keys fell to the floor.

"Shit," Spur heard. "I wasn't planning on this. Let's get the hell out of here."

"How?" the other man said. "The sheriff's out front, and there ain't no back way."

"We'll go out shooting. Come on!"

They ran to the door and kicked it open. Shots blasted and both men fell in seconds. Spur watched one of them roll over and groan before lying still. McCormick, his Colt still drawn and smoking, stepped over the bodies into the jail.

"You and me've got some talking to do," he said to Spur.

FOURTEEN

"I've already told you, Sheriff; I've never seen those men before." Spur slumped lower in his chair in the jail and dragged heavily on the hand-rolled smoke.

"That doesn't make sense. Are you trying to tell me two total strangers tried to break you out of jail?"

"Yes," Spur said. "As far as I can tell they were raiders. And just as the raiders got me in here, they were going to break me out."

"But why?" McCormick said, ignoring Spur's allegation.

"Think for a minute. As long as I'm in jail and everyone thinks I'm Rontrell, the raiders' hands are tied. Until I'm out of here they can't pull another raid."

"Makes sense."

"So they get me into jail, and then get me out, to be their scapegoat, to be the town's Rontrell. And even though no proof is offered to convince the law

111

that I'm Rontrell, the people of Fargo will believe it. Meanwhile the real Rontrell is above suspicion, free to move around the town and lead his raids. They probably would have killed me if they'd gotten me out of here and I would have conveniently disappeared.''

The sheriff was silent for a moment, then looked across his desk at Spur.

"Who the hell are you, Spur? You're not just passing through town; you're not an ignorant cowboy and you're not a lawman. Just who the hell are you?''

"Spur McCoy." He grinned at the Sheriff's exasperation.

"I'm not a bad judge of character and I realize that you're not Rontrell. But I have to hold you for twenty-four hours; that's the law.''

"At least we know there won't be any raids during that time," Spur said.

"Guess I'll keep you here. I'll have to watch you until I can let you go. Herman's got a hard knock on his head."

"He can't work?''

"Not for a day or so. Doc Thomas said he'll be fine after a short rest. I guess I'm stuck watching you until I free you.''

"You said twenty-four hours?'' Spur asked.

"Yeah. Should be around sunset. Just keep quiet and don't give me any trouble and you'll be free by sundown.''

"Sure," Spur said.

"I don't know what got into Zane's head," McCormick said, shaking his head. "You're no more

Rontrell than he is."

"That's right."

Spur went back to the cell and sat. McCormick shut the door and smiled. "Sundown'll be here before you know it."

"By the way, did you send someone out looking for Charlie Vendrick?"

"Who?"

"Charlie Vendrick, the raider I wounded and questioned last night."

"Oh yes; I seem to remember your mentioning something about that. I haven't had time yet." The sheriff's face was stiff; it was a lying face.

"I see," Spur said quietly. "And Jake Castle, the raider Vendrick named to me?"

"Jake Castle?"

"Yeah. Why don't you check up on him? It might pay to have the man watched."

"Spur, you never wore a badge, did you?"

He shrugged.

"Won't talk about it, will you? Fine. But if you're not Rontrell, you're sure as hell somebody, and I hope I find out who."

Spur smiled curtly and looked at the mud on his boots, thinking.

An hour after sundown McCormick let Spur out of his cell, promising to check up on Vendrick and Castle.

Spur went directly to Kelly's, glad that a sweet-faced woman had brought him dinner to his cell so he didn't have to waste time eating. Had Lila uncovered any information about Vendrick or Castle?

Spur searched the building fruitlessly, then asked the bartender if he knew Lila's whereabouts.

"She left for her room about two hours ago."

Spur thanked the man and headed for her boarding house. Once there he saw light shining beneath her door. He knocked and it was immediately opened.

"Spur," she said. "Thank God you're out of jail."

"I looked for you at the saloon," he said, entering her room.

"I didn't know how long you'd be in jail, so I decided to wait here."

"What about Vendrick and Castle?" Spur looked around for a bottle of whiskey.

"Vendrick hasn't been seen all day, not since early last night. I talked with his wife and she's afraid he's either run off like he always said he would, or that he's dead."

Spur sighed and then spied the whiskey. He walked to it. "What about Castle?"

"I don't know. I saw him in town today, but I couldn't run up and ask if he's a raider. If I could get him alone I think I could find out everything we need to know. He's been wanting me since his wife died. I can tell by the way he looks at me in the saloon. Maybe I could ask him some questions, after. . . ." Lila sighed. "No. Jake's not the type of man who'd slip up and start talking freely—not even in bed. He's too nervous, too sad."

"I see. You hear anything in town about either of them?" Spur collected two cups he found beside the bottle and took them and the whiskey to the bed, where he sat and poured the drinks. She sat next to him.

"No," Lila said. "I asked a friend of mine if he'd seen Charlie and he had, but that was days ago. No help there." She took the drink he offered, sipped it, and set it on the bedside table.

"At least I know that Vendrick told me his real name, and that he's dead. I don't know when his body will turn up; I'm sure the raiders hid it well." Spur set his glass on the beside table.

Lila frowned. "Come on, Spur. Forget the raiders for a while." She kissed his strong jaw and unbuttoned his flannel shirt, pulled it from his body, knocked his hat off his head, and ran her fingers through his chest hair, caressing his nipples.

"I've wanted you," she whispered. "I've wanted you so."

Spur felt his body flush with erotic heat as her hands dipped lower. He kissed her, gripping her head, thrusting his tongue savagely between her lips.

While they were kissing Spur rose. He pulled his head from hers and kicked off his boots, then lowered his pants. Lila stood motionless, smiling, as he undressed her. Moments later, their clothing entwined on the floor, Spur laid Lila on the bed and stared down at her.

He kissed her breasts and gently licked each nipple, then moved farther down her body with a trail of wet kisses. A moment later Lila cried out as Spur moved his head between her legs.

He felt her body shiver and then tense as he worked her over. Lila gave one more cry, then was silent. He slid onto her and gently ground his hips against hers, kissing her cheeks, eyes and lips, avoiding the inevitable.

"Oh Spur," Lila said breathlessly. "Come inside me now. Please, Spur!"

"Whatever you want." He gripped her hips, lifted them gently, positioned himself and drove into her body.

Lila's back arched and she sighed. Spur stopped then, reveling in the feeling, and held her tightly to him. He felt his own control shatter and he withdrew, then rammed back in and set up a furious tempo, while the bed squeaked softly beneath them.

Lila's hands caressed his neck, slid down his back, feeling the muscles there, and then gripped his buttocks. She pulled them to her with every thrust, trying to force him deeper within her.

Spur, tiring of the position, pulled out of her so quickly that she gasped.

"On your hands and knees," he said, his voice husky.

She stared at his gleaming erection, then nodded and moved into that position.

He plowed into her from behind, his thighs slapping against her buttocks, then grabbed her waist to steady himself. Spur hadn't pumped into her more than ten times when Lila's body shuddered and she threw her head back, her face alight with ecstasy.

He looked down, watching where their bodies joined, and increased the harshness of his strokes, banging so hard into her that he felt her bones.

Spur's body broke out in a thick sweat; his ears pounded and he closed his eyes as his pleasure increased tenfold. He finally erupted into her while the bed spun wildly and the wind rushed past his ears.

He leaned over Lila then, still within her, and his hands found her hanging breasts and his lips brushed the back of her shining neck. She moved, so Spur pulled out from her and dropped onto his back, then reached for Lila, who laid on him. They dissolved their fatigue in a passionate kiss while their heated bodies slipped together on the cool sheets.

Lila pulled her mouth from his, then placed a hand on each side of Spur's head and stretched like a cat in the morning sunlight.

"My God, Spur, you sure know how to give a woman all she can handle," she said, settling onto him.

"I try."

"I've never done it that way."

He looked up at her. "What way?"

"You know, with our bodies like that."

"You like it?"

"Of course, Spur. You don't hear any complaints, do you?"

She smiled and kissed his sweaty, stubble-covered neck, then pushed her tongue into his ear and gently nibbled on the lobe.

He felt his erection stir and grow to its fullest length. Lila pulled her mouth from his ear and pecked at his forehead, then reached down and gripped him.

"Looks like you're ready for seconds," she said.

"Could be. Are you?"

"That's a stupid question, Spur. You know me

better than that." She moved onto her knees, straddling his groin. She settled down, impaling herself on his erection, and sighed.

"Spur, you're a hell of a man."

"Don't talk, Lila. Work."

She frowned, then bobbed her body up and down, slowly circling her hips, making the most of the position.

Spur lay back, watching her, and smiled. Lila wasn't a crude saloon girl, but she was wise in the arts of love. Spur thought she was the best woman he'd had in years; they were perfectly suited to each other.

"What are you thinking about?" she asked, her breath coming in short gasps.

"Sex."

"How appropriate." She shook then, and her motions above him took on a more serious tone.

Spur felt his own pleasure mounting as she swayed above him, and when Lila cried out and her breasts flushed, Spur was nearing his own orgasm.

Lila slowed her motions, shaking her head, trying to recover from her climax as Spur took one of her buttocks in each hand, lifted them gently, and thrust up into her with breathtaking speed.

Lila's mouth hung open, puffing out her breath, while he rammed into her.

Spur raised her body even higher to thrust deeper into her, and she shivered as his tension and excitement grew to its peak, exploding in a moment of unbridled release.

Lila settled down onto him, her head thrown back, breathing deeply, and lifted a hand to pull the hair from her eyes.

Spur smiled up at her, waves of exhaustion flooding his body. She'd wear him out. But at least she'd gotten his mind off the raiders.

FIFTEEN

Spur edged through the saloon's crowd toward the bar. Once there he ordered a drink. Kelly's was packed. As he'd walked in several men turned to stare, and he'd ignored their gazes.

Word must have gone round that he was suspected of being Rontrell, Spur thought. That didn't bother him as long as no one decided to kill "Rontrell." He got his drink without a word from the bartender and turned, leaning against the bar, surveying the room.

Spur needed a lead; he'd have to question some people. Vendrick was dead, Castle out of sight. No one had seen him for some time. Someone must know something that could lead him to one of the raiders. If he could isolate just one member and follow him day and night, that one would lead him to the whole group.

He'd had Lila ask around about Jake Castle after they'd left her room, but no one had seen him. He'd hoped to use Castle as his target but couldn't if the man were hiding.

The man next to him turned and stared at Spur. He ignored him, then frowned. "You have something to say to me?" Spur asked.

"I hear you're Rontrell," the man said softly.

He was muscled, gritty, sunbrowned and evil smelling. His lips were fleshy, loose, disgusting.

"You heard wrong."

"Zane thinks you're Rontrell." The voice was so low that Spur had to bend forward to hear it.

"A lot of people think things."

He smiled. "That's right. You're looking into the raiders, ain't ya?" No one else in the saloon could hear the man's words.

"Could be." Spur kept his response as noncommittal as possible.

"Maybe I could help you."

"How?"

A cough. "Not here. Meet me behind the general store in ten minutes." The man turned his back to Spur.

An ambush arranged by the raiders? No. They wouldn't be that subtle. The man was cautious. Either way, Spur had no choice. He'd be at the general store.

He finished the drink and ordered another. As he did so, he noticed the man had left the bar. Perhaps he'd changed his mind, perhaps not. Spur downed the drink and left Kelly's, aware of the eyes watching him. He pushed through the batwing doors out into the night.

The general store. He was early, but the man was

probably already there. He turned to his left, passed the barber shop and a boarding house, and finally saw the general store two hundred feet ahead.

As he approached it Spur heard the sharp crack of a firearm from the general store's vicinity. He dashed to it, saw nothing in front and ran to the back. In a shadow lay a motionless, prone figure.

No one else was in sight. Spur bent and recognized the man from the bar. Spur touched his shirt; it was soaked with blood. Chest wounds like that were usually fatal; there wasn't much time. The man sputtered and coughed; he was attempting to talk. Spur propped him against the wall. The lips quivered in pain and effort as he delivered the message.

"The man in blue."

Fluid coughs staccatoed the words.

"A raider?" Spur hazarded.

The man nodded.

"He's the one who shot you?"

The head moved, but Spur couldn't distinguish a shake or nod.

"Who is he? Is he Rontrell?"

A convulsion racked the man's body. The head slumped forward. Spur raised it; the eyes stared at his, yellowish in the night air. They were lifeless.

Spur left the area quickly, unwilling to give the mayor another reason to have him locked up. The man in blue. A man dressed in blue. It was worth looking into.

"Is he dead?" Johnson asked, his fingers battering out a tattoo on the desk.

"I'm sure he is. I hit him square in the chest at

five feet."

"But did you check?"

The skinny man shook his head. "No. I didn't have time. I heard someone walking toward the store. I had to run before I was seen."

"We'll assume that he was dead, and that Spur got no information from him."

The man's eyes widened. "You think it was Spur who walked up?"

"Of course. Spur is intelligent. He generally knows which moves to make. You did well, Burns, watching Spur in Kelly's and eliminating any future problems with the other man. If only the mayor had been more sensible, like you." Johnson frowned. "Of all the stupid stunts, to have Spur locked up! He didn't realize that would tie our hands. At least McCormick released him." He shook his head and selected a pipe from the rack on his desk. "I'm going to have to have a talk with Zane. He's getting out of control, jeopardizing our plans. On your way back, stop by his place and tell him I want to see him. Now!"

"Yes, Mr. Johnson." The man hustled out of the room, leaving behind a thin cloud of gray dust.

Johnson shook his pipe, then moved his tobacco jar closer and packed the bowl. He was subtly losing his hold on Zane Evans. The man was striking out on his own, making decisions without consulting him. He'd have to see that the situation did not get out of hand.

Spur was becoming more of a problem, but Johnson had instructed his men well. Spur would be killed should he come too close to identifying any of the raiders.

True, he had no idea what, if anything, Vendrick had told him after the raid on the mayor's office, but whatever it was Spur hadn't moved on it, so it couldn't be too important. Sloppy work, Vendrick allowing himself to be caught that way.

Johnson tamped down hard on the bowl, struck a match and lit it, sucking the sweet smoke into his mouth. As he exhaled, he seemed to see the blueish smoke form into a woman's face in the air before him.

A woman. Lila Fairley. That was it; the key to ending part of the troubles. He'd been soft on Spur too long. It was time to get rid of him.

Spur ate with gusto the meal that Julie had prepared for him, and she stood and watched amusedly, while the peas, mashed potatoes and roast beef disappeared from the plain china plate.

"Julie," Spur said, after he'd pushed the plate away from him, "do you know a man in Fargo who dresses in blue?"

"A man who's dressed in blue?" She removed the plate and went to the counter. "Half of Fargo dresses in blue, but I can't seem to think of anyone in particular right now. Why? That seems a strange question, even from you, Spur." She sliced a freshly baked apple pie.

"Just wondering. I saw a man the other day and he was dressed in blue—pants, shirt, even a blue vest. I wondered who he was. He seemed to favor that color." Spur hoped Julie would accept the explanation; he couldn't reveal to her the actual reason for his question.

"Lots of men wear blue. I'm araid that isn't much to go on." She transferred a piece of pie to the small plate and took it to the table.

"I thought you might know someone who constantly wore blue."

"Was he well dressed? I mean, clean, expensive clothing?"

Spur shrugged. "You could say that."

"The first one who comes to mind—now that I've thought about it—is Farley. Farley Harris. But he moved out of Fargo last year."

"If you think of anyone else, I'd appreciate it." He dug his fork into the pie and ate a bite, smiled and took another.

"I hope I put enough sugar in it," Julie said. "I'm almost out and you know how expensive sugar is."

"It's fine."

He quickly finished the pie and stood. "Thanks for the dinner; I appreciate it."

"Running off again?" Julie asked, hands on her hips.

"Yes. I have to see someone."

"Just don't get yourself shot at again."

"Sorry about the window; I'll pay you for it."

"Nothing to worry about. I was going to replace that one anyway; it was cracked."

Spur shrugged. "All right. See you."

He left the kitchen and went directly to Lila's boarding house. Maybe he'd have better luck with her. He knocked but received no answer. She might be in the saloon. Spur walked there, an urgency slicing through his movements.

When he spotted her, Spur wordlessly took her hand and pulled her outside. She looked at him in surprise, but didn't speak as they moved from the saloon.

Finally Spur halted in a deserted area. "Spur, what is it?"

"Do you know anybody who always dresses in blue clothes?"

"Why?" she asked, her face curious in the moonlight.

"Never mind. Do you?"

"Yes, the first one I can think of Jim Fraser."

"Fraser. Where have I heard that name before?"

"Jim Fraser is Mayor Evans' clerk."

"Thanks, Julie."

"Look, Spur, what are you doing? Is this involved with the raiders again? You're using me for information and cutting me out of your confidence. Whoever you are, whatever you are, you can trust me." She put her arms around him, pulled him close, and kissed his lips quickly.

"I'm sorry, Lila."

He brushed his mouth to hers and broke from her hold.

"All right. But no one could say I haven't tried. I'll try to understand, Spur, but it'll be hard."

"I know. But it's the only way. Can I walk you back to the saloon?" he asked.

"No thanks. I think I'll get some sleep. See you, Spur." She turned and shuffled down the street.

Spur smiled. He had a name, Jim Fraser. Spur had to find him.

SIXTEEN

Spur had a good picture of Jim Fraser in his mind, though he'd seen the man for mere seconds before the raiders descended on the mayor's office last night. Fraser was tall, thin, pale, and looked as if he'd never worked with his hands.

As Spur pictured Fraser he realized the clerk had been dressed in blue—britches, shirt and vest—and wondered why he hadn't remembered.

He took out his pocket watch and checked the time; nearly midnight. Spur moved down Main Street to the mayor's office, where light still burned in the front window. The mayor wouldn't be there this late at night, but maybe Fraser would.

Spur took the risk. He had to get another glance at Fraser. As he entered the office the clerk looked up from his desk, rubbed his eyes and put his pen down.

"Can I help you?" The voice was high, whining.

"Yes. Is the mayor around?"

"No. He's home for the day. You could try in the morning, about eight."

"Thanks."

He paused to look at Fraser a moment longer, then left and shut the door behind him. Fraser's face hadn't hinted at his feelings about Spur; the man would be a perfect poker player.

Spur remembered the events of last night's raid on the mayor's office. Evans had opened the door and Fraser had walked out, then the raiders were there, and Spur had pushed the mayor into the office and followed. He'd forgotten about Fraser, but apparently the man hadn't been wounded. But then the raiders wouldn't kill one of their own without good cause.

Spur found a shadowy place across the street from the mayor's office and sat there watching. Fraser would have to leave eventually.

Not long afterward he did. The light went out in the window. Spur stood slowly, keeping well within the blackness, watching as Fraser left the building, locked the door and moved down the street.

Spur followed, ducking into shadows or behind objects, matching Fraser's speed but staying about a hundred feet behind. Finally Fraser turned onto a side street and moved out of Spur's sight. Spur hurried across and picked up Fraser again on Pine. The clerk went to a small, dismal building, unlocked the door and stepped inside. Soon light glowed through a window. Fraser must be home. Spur sighed, stood leaning against a fencepost, and removed his bag of fixings from his pocket. At least the night wasn't freezing cold.

At dawn Spur stretched, his joints cracking in the chilled wind, his cheeks numb. He stuffed his hands into his pockets. Fraser hadn't moved from his home; the light had been quenched minutes after he'd arrived. Spur knew Fraser would be rising soon, and didn't want the clerk to see him watching, so he prepared to move as soon as Fraser appeared.

Half an hour later, when Spur's feet were aching from standing still, Fraser pushed his door open and stepped outside, his breath frosting before him. Spur immediately launched into a casual stroll, glancing back once at Fraser to determine his direction. Fraser moved north, seemingly back to his office.

Spur hurried around the block in time to see Fraser cross Main Street and move on. He caught up with the man and, from the opposite side of the street, saw Fraser approach a huge two-story house on Elm Street surrounded by pines and a high wrought-iron fence. The house was grotesquely out of place in Fargo and made the rest of the neighborhood seem impoverished.

To Spur's surprise, Fraser didn't climb the steps to the massive double doors, but instead untied a palomino that stood at a hitching post in front, climbed on and rode quickly away.

Spur cursed the man for his unexpected action, ran to Main Street, got his own horse and galloped off into the same direction, hping to catch sight of Fraser.

Luck was with him; Fraser headed west out of town. Spur's brain jarred—that direction seemed significant to the raiders. He followed some distance behind, off the trail, but with little cover. Spur hoped Fraser wouldn't be expecting to be followed and therefore wouldn't be on his guard.

The clerk stopped fifteen minutes outside of town. Spur let his horse graze on a grassy area near a tiny seasonal stream, and moved up to watch Fraser's actions.

He saw the man take a blue handkerchief from his pocket and tie it to a tree branch that hung over the trail—the same tree he'd seen the other day.

Then without hesitation Fraser rode back toward town. Spur climbed onto his horse and leisurely followed. He was sure of the clerk's actions now. He'd return to the house, tie up the horse, and go do work as if nothing was out of the ordinary.

Perhaps nothing was. Fraser was a raider. His job, Spur surmised, was to tie on the handkerchief, probably to announce a meeting. That's easy—Rontrell's calling a meeting. But where? When? What time?

Spur tied up his horse in front of the Wyler Hotel and ate a bite of breakfast from Julie, then proceeded directly to the mayor's office. He wasn't surprised to see Fraser sitting behind his desk.

"Ah yes, Mr. McCoy. The mayor's in and he's eager to see you."

"Thanks." He walked past the and followed a corridor to a door at its end. He knocked, then entered.

Though he wasn't keen on facing the mayor, Spur

132

knew it would be a good thing to do. He'd have to choose his words carefully to prevent an outbreak of the man's temper, though.

"Mr. McCoy. I heard you wanted to see me," Evans said, looking up from his desk, where a thick book lay opened before him.

"Yes. I don't much like anyone's blackening my name—especially when it's to accuse me of being Rontrell."

To Spur's surprise the man smiled.

"I'm sorry about that. I really am. I don't know what got into me—I guess it was that raid last night. I don't have to tell you I wasn't prepared for it—and apparently Rontrell wasn't either. He must have been expecting me to be indoors, not standing in front of my office. I want to thank you for shoving me inside here. You quite probably saved my life."

"Anytime," Spur said evenly.

The man considered him, then shrugged gently. "After you rode off on Ned's horse, I got this crazy idea you were Rontrell and had planned the raid. Then for some reason you changed your mind and saved me, and afterward you rode off to talk to your men." The mayor shrugged. "I know now that was a damnfool thing to think, and I apologize."

"No harm done—at least, no permanent damage." What was Evans' game? Why was he acting so shamed, so embarrassed?

"So if that's what you've come here to talk about, I guess I deserve whatever you give me."

Spur knew that the man was lying, and badly at that, but he decided to play along.

"Anybody can make a mistake. I guess you made

133

yours."

Zane Evans smiled and wiped his brow. "Somehow that makes me feel worse. But I hope you'll accept my apology, Mr. McCoy."

"Sure. And check your facts before you have the sheriff arrest me again."

"I will. I promise."

He left the office and went past Fraser silently. The clerk didn't look up as Spur closed the door.

Spur stood outside the mayor's office thinking. The meeting would be in the evening, probably around sundown. Working men couldn't get away during the day. While Fraser was worth watching, Spur's real ace was the meeting—if there was to be one.

He realized with a dull suddenness that he hadn't slept for two days. Spur went to his hotel and stretched out on his bed, watching cloudy sunlight poke in through the shot-out window until he slept.

At three that afternoon Spur stood opposite the mayor's office, engaging Lila in a mock conversation, glancing at the door through which Fraser would exit. Moments earlier he'd had Lila make sure Fraser was there, by having her stop in to say hello to the clerk, whom she'd seen a few times, as she revealed to Spur. He hadn't told her why he was watching Fraser and Lila hadn't pressed him for a reason.

At three-thirty, when Lila was beginning to complain about her feet, Fraser left his office and went to Elm Street. Lila and Spur followed at some distance and reached the corner just as Fraser disappeared into the imposing house.

"That's Clint Johnson's home," Lila said.

"I met him in Kelly's, didn't I?"

"Yes. He's the richest man in town."

"I remember. I wonder how he's mixed up with Fraser."

"They've been friends for years; Jim's alone. He never married and he lost his parents when he was a boy, so Clint and Francine took him in almost like a son.

"Francine? Clint's wife?"

"No, his sister. I guess Jim likes the attention. He's a loner, never stops by the saloon, just works his job and goes home, or to see the Johnsons. I felt sorry for him once, so I saw him a few times, even got him into my bed, but he was so innocent I felt like I was robbing the cradle. I still see him now and then, but he's a strange man, Spur."

"I know."

Fraser left Johnson's house and untied the same horse, but led it on foot to his own place while Spur and Lila followed.

"Spur, I'm exhausted. Think I'll go to my room and rest. See you later, okay?"

"Sure."

She left him with a smile.

Spur knew, if there was to be a raiders' meeting tonight, they would head out west. There was no sense watching Fraser's home for the next hour or so. He went to his hotel, dodged Julie's questions, had her make him a sandwich and downed it with a quart of milk, then got his horse and situated himself near the outskirts of town, hiding behind a livery, on the trail heading west.

At dusk the first few men rode out. Spur recognized none of them in the deepening twilight, but he discerned Fraser's mount and followed shortly after the last of the nearly ten men had passed him.

When the raiders came to the handkerchief signal they rode past without pause and continued down the trail for five minutes, then turned south.

Spur followed cautiously, barely able to make out their forms in the deepening twilight. The sun soon was down fully and light was scarce, but the horse had little trouble picking its way through the brush and few ditches where winter rains had cut rivulets through the soft earth.

Five minutes later he smelled smoke and heard an occasional voice ahead of him. He'd lost sight of the raiders earlier but had followed a bright star to maintain his direction, trusting that they'd ridden straight without veering off. Apparently this was true.

The noises grew louder, and Spur realized he wasn't hearing words but whoops. The scent of smoke was pungent now, but he could see no flames or even a glow. Where were the raiders?

He tied his horse to a straggly tree and walked cautiously ahead; the sounds grew louder. It wasn't until he was nearly on top of them that he spied the fire and the raiders thirty feet in front of him.

They'd positioned themselves behind a small hill that had, at some time in the past, been cut in half, leaving a sharp cliff which afforded them complete privacy from two directions.

Spur shifted his eyes beyond the raiders, attempting to sum up the area's strategic positioning. Dark masses he took for trees dotted the other sides, as well as an even darker spot that must be a dense copse of them. Scantly cover, but adequate if a few men rode from that direction.

Spur dropped to his belly, testing the cliff and deciding it would hold his weight. On his approach he hadn't seen a guard on duty in the area, so he felt safe while he inspected the men.

Due to the flickering firelight and his distance from them, Spur couldn't be sure of their exact number, but he knew it was under ten. All wore masks. They milled around the small fire, drinking coffee. Spur thought he saw Fraser but he couldn't be sure.

He glanced to their right and saw, after his eyes had recovered from the fire's glare, the horses tied up among the trees.

Though he was near, Spur couldn't make out any words. They were either mumbled or overpowered by the wind that blew stiffly from the north. Spur would have to move closer to listen to their conversations. As he backed from the cliff's edge he felt the earth move beneath him. A two-foot-square chunk of the cliff broke free and tumbled down.

He scrambled back as it fell, jumped to his feet and ran for his horse. Without waiting to see if the raiders knew of his presence he rode off toward the dim lights of Fargo, cursing the cliff and his trust in it.

SEVENTEEN

Rontrell sent men in search of an intruder, but thought they'd find nothing. Sure enough, no one had been on the cliff. In any case, he wouldn't let the incident spoil his plans. Nothing could stop him now. When he'd calmed the men he told them of their next mission.

"Gentlemen, we embark tonight on a mission of the greatest importance. Tonight at midnight we shall ride into Fargo and abduct Lila Fairley."

There were no gasps of surprise, no flinching among his men. Rontrell smiled at his troops; they were completely under his control.

"Lila Fairley has been known to see Spur McCoy, and I believe is aiding him in his attempts to break up our group. This I cannot allow. She will finish work at midnight at Kelly's Saloon. As she's leaving we'll abduct her and bring her here. At that time I'll give you further instructions. Any questions?"

The men shook their heads; they were quiet, listening, thinking.

"Good. We'll ride into Fargo silently; no shooting or yelling. After taking up our positions we'll wait until she leaves the saloon, then take her and ride straight back here. Shoot anyone who moves to stop or harm us. The objective of this mission is to bring Lila back here—alive. Is that clear?"

The men mumbled their acknowledgment.

"Good."

"Mr. Rontrell?" one man said.

"Yes?"

"Are you gonna let us . . . I mean, are you going to let us pleasure her?"

Rontrell grunted softly. "We'll see. I haven't decided on that yet. It depends on her actions and behavior when we take her. That satisfy you?"

"Yes, Mr. Rontrell. It does."

"Good. We've got four hours to kill. Do whatever you want but don't stray from the fire. And I'm posting an extra guard. You—" he said, pointing to a man,—"up on the ridge, in the brush. I don't want even that direction unwatched. Go now, and keep the noise down."

Rontrell glanced away from the fire at Jake Castle, who stood with arms crossed on his chest, staring at him.

Spur was still cursing his luck as he ordered a rye in Kelly's. That cliff had to give way just when he was lying belly down on it, watching the raiders.

At least he knew where they met. The site was perfect for their plans: virtually invisible from the surrounding area, even with a fire at night. Only the keenest eyes—those which were specially looking for something—could see the thin column of smoke that rose from the blaze.

Spur saw Lila at the piano, plunking out a tune, while a chunky man stood beside her, leering openly. The secret service man didn't want to interrupt her, so he finished his drink and ordered another, thinking of Rontrell and his next move.

Jake Castle stood as Rontrell called the men together at the fire. It was twenty minutes to midnight. Rontrell went over the plan again, then walked with them to the horses.

Rontrell wanted this to be a clean, quiet, quick raid, Castle thought. He swung up into his saddle, feeling excitement stir inside him as he dug his heels into the horse's sleek flanks. Not only emotional excitement, but physical. The hardness in his pants moved against the saddlehorn as they rode toward Fargo. Jake couldn't stop thinking about Lila. Hopefully Rontrell would let the men have her. Finally he thought, I'll have her, and she won't be able to do a damn thing about it.

They rode hard toward Fargo and in less than twenty minutes arrived at the outskirts of town. Few people were on the streets this late, due to the fear the raiders had inspired, Jake thought smugly. A few men trailed into saloons, but otherwise Main Street was quiet.

"Let's go," Rontrell said.

They moved into the town as silently as possible, wanting to attract no attention. Rontrell had his men spread out in a wide half circle around the saloon's entrance. He pulled his watch out and surveyed its face; Jake judged it to be midnight exactly, and he knew Lila was a woman who left work on time.

Jake sat uneasily on his mount. What if something went wrong? He fought the thought but couldn't deny it. This was his second raid, and the last one had failed miserably; Spur had intervened. This one would be better, he promised himself.

One minute passed. Two. And another. Jake saw Rontrell staring at the doors, as if he were willing Lila to come through them and fall into the trap. Rontrell was closer than the rest, next to the wall, a foot from the doors. As Lila came out of them Rontrell would reach down, grab her, and ride.

Why didn't she leave? Jake wiped a sheen of sweat from his forehead, despite the chill in the air. He felt his muscles tighten. Where was the woman?

The sound of footsteps jarred his brain. He looked at the doors. A pair of feet, encased in women's boots, came into view below them. Lila Fairley walked to the batwing doors, paused, and turned.

"I'll see you later tonight, Spur. Just don't lose all your money. I want you to buy me a drink tomorrow."

She walked from the saloon, looking at the ground, oblivious of the men gathered around her.

Jake watched in intense interest as Rontrell reached down, grabbed Lila under her arms, and hoisted her onto his horse, seating her in front of him. She screamed once before he wrapped a hand over her mouth and spurred his horse. With his men following, the raiders were out of town in less than a minute and no one could have known they had been there.

When they were safely away from Fargo Rontrell released his hand from Lila's mouth. She remained silent, then turned her head to speak to Rontrell. Jake rode nearer so that he could hear the woman's words.

"What the hell do you think you're doing?"

"I think I'm taking you by force," Rontrell said.

"Why? For what reason? What have I done to you?"

"Nothing. It's what you've done against me."

Even in the moonlight, her face a mask of confusion and growing anger, Jake was surprised at Lila's beauty.

"I don't know what you're talking about. Stop this horse and put me down."

"No. You'll have to come with me."

"Where are you taking me?"

"Can't tell you that."

"And are you going to kill me? If so, you should have done that at the saloon, because I'll do everything in my power to get away from you, Rontrell!"

He laughed. "So you know who I am."

"Of course."

"But you don't know why I had you taken?"

"No."

"You were helping Spur."

"Spur? What makes you think I've been helping him? All right, I've been going to bed with him, but how's that helping him?"

"Shut up," Rontrell said. "This is boring me."

143

Jake rode along to their meeting place, waiting for the moment when he could take Lila and spread her lily-white legs wide. . . .

Minutes later they were at the fire, which had died low. Jake quickly threw wood on it and flames leaped high with the fresh fuel. Rontrell brought the struggling Lila closer to the blaze and posted two guards.

"Okay, Rontrell," she said. "What are you going to do with me?"

He smiled. "Pleasure you."

She shook her head. "No."

"You are not in any position to tell me what I am or am not going to do." He turned to the men who were circled around him "I need four men to hold her down," he snapped.

Jake jumped forward; he was one of the four.

"Rip her clothes off," Rontrell said, as he unbuttoned his pants and began working himself to a full erection with his fist.

"No!" Lila said.

"Don't tell me you're going to pretend this is your first time," Rontrell said.

Jake's skinny fingers slipped under the neckline of her bodice and jerked downward violently. The material ripped and exposed her white chemise. With another fast motion Jake had that off, and her beautiful white breasts were in full view.

Rontrell grunted and his fist moved faster at his crotch as he looked at her. Another man tore the rest of her dress away, and Jake felt excitement flush through him as he saw the rich, lustrous black triangle between her legs. The firelight played on her body, giving it an almost supernatural quality.

"Hold her legs and arms down steady," Rontrell said, slipping his pants down, his huge erection standing out in front of him.

Jake and the other three men did as they were ordered, until Lila could barely move. She cried out once, then closed her eyes as Rontrell knelt between her widespread legs. Jake didn't attempt to hide his stare as Rontrell positioned himself and thrust into Lila's body.

She screamed again and thrashed but the men pinned her down firmly. Rontrell held himself up with his hands and knees and began pumping into her.

"Someone lift up her ass!" he said, without missing a stroke.

One stuck a boot under her and Rontrell smiled as his strokes plunged deeper into her.

"You fucking bitch!" he said. "I don't know why I'm even bothering. It's just that every other man in town's been in there . . . why shouldn't I?"

He grunted and thrust more swiftly, sweat springing out on his back and shoulders. Jake felt his own erection throb in his pants but ignored it; he'd have his chance later.

The firelight caught the look of ecstasy on Rontrell's face while he thrust into her twice, then again, while his body jerked and his head swung back. A low cry strangled from his throat, and he collapsed onto her, his torso rising and falling steadily with his labored breath.

After a moment he roused and stood, then pulled up his pants.

"Any of you who want her can have her."

Lila's face was cool, but Jake thought he saw a tear squeeze from her left eye.

The man who'd held her left leg moved swiftly between them, claiming the next turn. The rest of the men scrambled for positions in line, and Jake went along with them, coming up fourth.

He saw Rontrell standing not far away.

"Mr. Rontrell?" he said.

"What, kid?"

"What are you going to do with her?"

"Hell, I don't know."

"Do you think maybe she'll come over to our side? Think she'll join us? Everybody knows she's sex happy. Maybe if we keep her busy she won't leave."

Rontrell turned to Jake and nodded. "Could be. It would be better; I don't want to kill a woman, but she knows too much about us. I have nothing against her personally, except that she's been helping Spur. Maybe you're right, kid. Maybe we could turn her to our side. When you boys are through with her we'll see."

Jake nodded. He heard a short, piercing cry that signaled the man's orgasm. The line moved up a moment later and Jake sighed, arms crossed on his chest, waiting his turn.

Seemingly moments later Jake knelt between her legs. He looked down at her; her eyes were shut, her head to her side. He unbuttoned his fly, pulled out his erection, and pushed it into her.

146

EIGHTEEN

Spur stood in the saloon and looked up from his drink. Had he heard a scream? Probably not. It could have been the wind, but the place was so noisy he couldn't be sure. He'd better check. Lila had just left; maybe she'd run into trouble.

Cursing, he moved across the bar and went outside. At the end of Main Street he saw several riders disappearing from sight.

Spur ran to his mount and followed. The raiders! Had they taken Lila as she came out of the saloon? He had to know. The men were gone but they were headed west, probably toward their hideout.

Spur rode fast and hard, and soon had turned off the trail toward their meeting place. When he smelled smoke he circled wide, avoiding the cliff, and presently saw the fire and the men. He tied the horse to a tree and froze; something snapped in the distance.

A guard? Spur was sure of it. The man moved through the trees until Spur saw him; he was alone, but armed. Silently Spur stepped behind an oak and waited until the guard was a foot from him, then jumped out and slammed the butt of his Colt hard onto the man's head. He slumped to the earth with a faint grunt.

Spur stripped the belt off the man and used it to secure his hands, then gagged him with his handkerchief mask. He also took the man's weapon and stuck it under his belt.

That done, Spur edged from tree to tree, nearing the fire and the raiders, until he had a clear picture of the scene. Lila lay on her back in front of the fire while a man pumped between her legs. Several others stood in a line next to her.

He moved closer, his body concealed behind a thick pine. Lila's head rotated in circles in the dust as the man plowed into her. It looked as if she were drugged, but Spur recognized the signs of sexual excitement. Lila was enjoying it!

The raiders had taken her to the fire and were now sexually using her. Surely she couldn't have gone willingly; but she wasn't fighting. No one was holding her down; she just lay there.

Perhaps she was humoring them until she found an avenue of escape. It was something Lila could do. For the time being Spur could forget Lila and think about the raiders.

He had the urge to blast them with his Winchester, but knew he couldn't kill all of them before he was himself wounded or killed. Besides, he didn't want to risk injuring Lila. He either had to pick off as many as he could now, and ride off safely, knowing he'd lessened the raiders' ranks, or go back to town, gather up a posse and the sheriff, and come back.

Before he could decide which course to choose he heard a crack behind him and whirled around to see a man standing there.

As he started to draw, a rifle's muzzle pressed into his crotch. He froze and stared into the steel-blue eyes of the gunman.

"You move and I'll blow your balls to bits, Spur." He jabbed the muzzle into Spur's groin, sending shock waves of pain through his body. "Rontrell! Mr. Rontrell! I've got Spur!" The man unholstered Spur's Colt, removed the weapon he'd taken from the guard, and knocked the Winchester to the ground. "Walk. Turn around and go to the fire. And don't try nothing, you're outnumbered fifteen to one."

Spur turned and did as the man said. He hadn't seen the second man on watch. Rontrell was being careful, he realized too late.

As they approached the fire Spur counted fifteen men present. Lila still lay on the ground, her eyes closed, while a man sweated over her.

"Hurry up," the man at the head of the line said. "I want my piece before Rontrell breaks this up."

A tall man walked up to Spur and put his hands on his hips.

"Spur, how good of you to join our little party. But then, I suppose you've fucked Lila more than once already, haven't you?"

"Yes," Spur said. "Why should you care?"

"I don't. I wondered if she satisfied you, that's all."

"She could satisfy any man. Did she satisfy you?"

Rontrell slammed his fist into Spur's chin without warning. Spur checked the impulse to return the blow.

"She did. But it doesn't matter now; I don't care about her." He paused. "I didn't think you would purposely provoke me, McCoy. I thought you were too intelligent for that."

"Oh, have we met?" Spur realized that something about the man was familiar. He couldn't place him. Who?

He ruled out the sheriff; McCormick was taller and thinner. The mayor? No.

"Not in this guise," Rontrell said, answering his question. "But yes, we have met. In town. Don't worry; I won't spoil your fun of discovering my identity. Perhaps that will show just how effective a government man you are."

"What makes you think I work for the state?" Spur asked, purposely directing the question away from the federal government.

"It's written in everything you do. We know you're here to clean up the raiders. I'm afraid that won't be possible."

"Why not?"

"Because you'll be dead." Rontrell was silent for a moment, then raised a hand. "Spur, you fought in the Great War, didn't you?"

"That's right."

"North or South?"

"I can't remember," Spur said with a straight face. He glanced at Lila; she was watching him curiously.

"But you must; it is imperative. Not that I'll explain why, but it just might save your life. Of course, there is a possibility that you're lying; that you didn't fight, that you hid in a hole somewhere like a coward until the shooting halted."

Spur wasn't going to let the man's tactics make him break down and talk. Could Rontrell be bringing up an old grudge? Was that what had started these raids—the Civil War?

"A pity; I thought you would tell me," Rontrell said after several moments of silence. "But no matter now. I shall have you executed. In fact, I could kill you and Lila together; that would be amusing."

The man on top of Lila stopped and looked up at Rontrell, then stood, while Lila rose to her feet beside him, naked.

"Don't think you could kill me and get away with it," Lila said, the color coming back into her cheeks and venom filling her voice. "Do you think your men would let you kill their girl?"

There were a few comments from the raiders. Rontrell looked at them while Lila approached him, her hips swinging gently. She laid a hand on the slight bulge at his crotch and rubbed slowly.

"Was I so bad? Wouldn't you like to get inside me again? Rontrell, I like servicing your boys. Why don't you let me join you? I'd be a good girl."

Rontrell spat at her feet. She withdrew her hand.

"Why should I? You're nothing special. You're just a piece of meat. A piece of fuck meat."

Spur saw Lila's eyes harden then. In the firelight her face flushed and she turned away, walking back

151

to the blaze.

"Yes, that would be nice. The two of you together, stark naked, shot to death. I could leave you as a calling card on Preacher Watkin's front porch! Maybe that would make the old shit curl up and die!"

A few of the raiders laughed, but others were silent.

Spur could see how close Rontrell was to losing control over his men; he was going too far for some of them.

"Shit, don't worry, boys. I'm not going to hurt Lila. Just trying to keep her in line. She's a good girl and we'll use her whenever we want. But Spur's another story. Not that I'd get anything out of killing him; he's done nothing to me yet. But he will if I let him live. So we'll kill him tonight before he can hurt us."

"And the girl?" a man asked quietly.

"Lila will live. But if she ever opens her mouth about us, we'll cut her to pieces and feed her to the vultures. I'll need a firing squad for the execution of Spur. Any volunteers?"

This seemed to lift the men's spirits, and many raised their hands.

"Shit, can't we wait until we've all had Lila?" one of the men in line asked.

"All right, that's fair." He pointed to two men. "You two watch Spur. Don't take your eyes off him even long enough to take a piss. I don't trust him. If he escapes both of you are dead. Understood?"

"Yes, sir!" the men said simultaneously.

"Back there," one of them said. Spur moved until

he was up against a tree. His hands were tied behind the trunk with a length of rope.

It was an uncomfortable position, but Spur knew he could work the rope free if he had enough time. The man's request also allowed him the opportunity to think out his course of action. He knew it wouldn't be easy, but that had never stopped him before.

From where he was standing, with both men watching him, he could just barely see Lila by straining his neck. The fire, with Lila and the men, was to his extreme right. He heard a short feminine cry and wondered if Lila were fighting the men; maybe Rontrell's speech had awakened her, or perhaps she was tired of playing along.

Spur sighed. He knew Lila had been bluffing when she offered to take care of all Rontrell's men for him if he let her live. She was smart enough to make the bluff. When he got out of this he'd take her where she couldn't be found, then plan how to stamp out the raiders forever.

NINETEEN

Spur stood quietly, leaning against a tree, hoping his two guards wouldn't notice that he was delicately, slowly moving his fingers and wrists.

He heard the men working out their lusts on Lila's body but shut it out of his mind; it broke his concentration. He had managed to loosen the knots around his wrists and was now working to get more slack.

He heard a short cry from Lila and wondered if she'd been hurt. At least Rontrell would spare her. That was one thing he could say for the man.

Rontrell. He'd said they'd met before, but he couldn't be the mayor or the sheriff; who else in Fargo had Spur met? He twisted his head and saw Rontrell, his back to him, staring at the stars and the moon. There had been that man in Kelly's Saloon, but he'd been short; Rontrell was nearly six feet tall.

Who else of importance had he met? Spur stared at Rontrell's back. The man who owned the biggest house in Fargo—the only other man Spur had met, aside from Fraser.

Clint Johnson.

Yes, it had to be. Same general size, same manner, same arrogance. The voice was lower, harsher, but that was easily faked. Rontrell had to be Clint Johnson.

Spur worked against the rope, trying to force the knots to enlargen slightly so that he could slide his wrists out of them. Then he'd grab Lila and they'd leave.

He wouldn't mention to Rontrell that he knew who he was; let him think his secret was safe. When Spur got back to town and informed the sheriff of Rontrell's identity, Clint Johnson might well become a man without a town; he couldn't be seen in either personality, Rontrell or Johnson, without being killed. That could wreck his band of raiders.

Spur twisted his face in pain as he tried to wrench his wrists free of the ropes.

One of the men watching him rose from his squat and came toward the bound Spur. "Hey, whatcha doin!" he asked, his eyes dark.

"Trying to get comfortable," Spur said. "These damn ropes are cutting into my wrists."

The man smiled. "Aw, ain't that too bad? You just stand there and don't squirm so much. You'll be dead soon enough." The guard laughed and returned to his position six feet from Spur.

The other guard had dozed off, leaning against a tree. Spur manipulated the ropes for another moment and suddenly one loop swung off his left hand; it was free. In a matter of seconds the other hand was mobile, and he held the ropes for a minute behind him, maintaining the illusion that he was still bound, thinking that the ropes could also be useful.

The only man that glanced at him was the guard. Rontrell and the rest of the men were busy watching Lila and her sexual partners. If he could take care of this guard without waking the other, he could have a chance.

To get the man closer to him, Spur pretended to try to free himself from the ropes, exaggerating his movements, while deftly switching the line to his right hand, reading it for use.

The guard looked at him again, rose and came within two feet of Spur. "I told you to stop squirming. What's the matter with you, don't you like my knots?"

Spur heard the grunts grow louder from the fire. The guard was close enough. In a swift motion Spur swung the rope up and then down around the man's neck. The guard dropped his Smith & Wesson and choked as Spur tightened the rope. In less than thirty seconds he slumped to the ground. The man was unconscious. Spur bound and gagged him, took the weapon and moved the body out of the way.

Spur heard a noisy climax issuing from the fire. He ran to the sleeping second guard, knocked him hard on the head with the Smith & Wesson, then lowered his kerchief to act as a gag. Two down, Spur thought grimly.

Rontrell still stood with his back to him. There

were no men between him and the raiders' leader.

Spur found his rifle and Colt on the earth; he slung the rifle on his back and gripped the Colt firmly. He steathily made his way to Rontrell, knowing the man could turn at any second and see him. He had to hurry; no time for fancy stalking or tricky movements.

Spur silently walked to within three feet of Rontrell and pressed the muzzle of his Colt against the man's back, then threw an arm around Rontrell's neck. The man cried out in surprise.

"All you men throw your weapons down," Spur shouted. "Now! In front of me!"

He felt Rontrell shake as his men faced him, staring. "Do what he says!" the leader screamed. "Do what he says!"

Spur pressed the muzzle more sharply against Rontrell's back when the men didn't immediately carry out his orders. "Throw your weapons down!" he yelled.

One man started, then seconds later there was a small pile of guns near Rontrell's feet.

"Bring me a horse," Spur said.

A man disappeared and returned with a horse, leading it in front of Rontrell and Spur.

"That's close enough," Spur said, recognizing it as the bay he'd rented in town. "Move back." The man did. "Lila, come here," he said. She rose from the ground, without dusting herself off or trying to hide her nakedness, and walked to him.

"Get on!" he said. She mounted, wincing as she slid into the saddle. "Move back. I'm getting in front." She nodded and moved.

158

Spur shoved Rontrell near the horse, then jabbed the Colt savagely in his back. "Don't anyone move till I'm out of sight," Spur said. He jumped onto the horse and raked his spurs hard against her flanks. She bolted from the fire and out into the darkness. Spur felt a slug streak past him in the air but it did no damage.

They were soon galloping across open country. Spur realized they were heading the wrong way, so he circled back and finally saw the lights of Fargo before them. He had no idea what the time was, but it must be near dawn.

"Spur, I'm freezing," Lila said, behind him.

He removed his coat and gave it to her. "This should help somewhat."

"Thanks."

He felt her putting it on behind him, then her hands once again gripped his waist.

"Are they following us?" he asked.

"No, I don't think so. I can't see them," Lila said in his ear after a short pause.

"Good. I hoped they wouldn't."

Soon the first light began staining the eastern sky. They rode into Fargo.

"I'll take you to my hotel," Spur said. "You can stay there for a while. It's not safe in your room."

"All right, Spur. God, I'm glad you showed up back there." Her voice sounded dreamy. "I tried to act like I was enjoying it but it hurts, Spur. It really does!"

"You'll have to spend some time resting up, but soon you'll be back to normal. It could have been much worse. They could have killed you."

"Don't even mention that."

Spur reined in the horse in front of the Wyler Hotel, swung off the saddle, and helped Lila down. They quickly went inside and no one saw them as he ushered her to his room and closed the door.

Spur lit the lamp, though dawn was spilling through the windows, had her take off his coat and handed her his other flannel shirt.

"Put this on," he said. She dressed and he kissed her forehead.

"I'm very tired," she said.

"Sleep." He took her to his bed and she lay down. Spur kissed her again. "I have to leave for a few minutes."

"Where are you going?" Her eyes were half closed.

"Outside to make sure we'll be safe. I don't want the raiders coming over here and starting it all over again. I'll be back in a few minutes. Stay here and don't open the door for anyone. I'll lock it and use my key. Okay?"

"All right." She settled down onto the bed. Spur lowered the flame, went into the hall and locked the door, then walked down the stairs—where he met Julie.

"What's happening?" she asked, staring at him.

"Nothing."

"But I thought I heard a woman's voice," she said suspiciously.

"You did. Lila Fairley."

Julie eyes went wide and her cheeks colored.

"It's not what you think," Spur said.

"Tell me what I'm thinking," she said defiantly.

"She was kidnapped from work and raped by the raiders."

"Oh dear God," Julia said, her hand rising to her mouth.

"I followed them, found her, and took her back here. Fortunately they didn't try to follow us. I'm just going out to make sure we'll be all right here. I don't think Rontrell will give us any trouble in town. But just to make sure, I'm going to look outside."

"I see. I'm sorry, Spur, but I—"

He cut her off gently. "What are you doing up this early?"

She blinked. "Just going out to collect the things for breakfast. I have to buy two dozen eggs and a gallon of milk."

"At dawn?" Spur asked.

"Every morning. Owning a hotel's not exactly easy living."

"You be careful, and keep an eye out for the raiders."

"You don't have to tell me twice, Spur. I will. And I'm sorry for what I thought about you and Lila."

"Don't mention it. You had no way of knowing."

She nodded and went down the stairs slowly, then disappeared into the kitchen.

Spur went outside and checked the perimeter of the hotel, looked at his horse, and moved it down the street to the front of Lila's boarding house. If the raiders knew it was his horse, maybe that would throw them off. That done, with no one in sight, Spur went back into the hotel. He used his key in the door and found Lila sleeping fitfully. He smiled and sat, had a glass of rye, and yawned.

He didn't want to sleep. He kept his eyes open and watchful as dawn brightened into day, and sunlight streamed in through the broken window.

An hour later, Spur caught himself dozing. He stood, stretched, and looked at the peacefully sleeping Lila. He smiled and was pacing the floor, thinking about Clint Johnson and his reasons for having formed the raiders, when he coughed. Then he smelled it—smoke! Not the sweet, pungent scent of a campfire, but smoke from a killer blaze.

Was it nearby? Spur looked out the window but could see no fire anywhere near. He remembered the Drake and Mason blaze that had occurred the day he arrived in Fargo—Johnson's handiwork.

The scent grew stronger, and Spur finally saw smoke curling in beneath his door. He went to the door and touched the knob. It was warm, but not hot. He gripped it, turned the knob and pulled the door inward.

The hall was murky, layers of gray smoke hanging in the air. In the distance, near the middle of the hall, he could see the shadows of wildly leaping flames, and a dull orangish glow flickered onto the walls.

Spur turned to Lila and shook her roughly.

She woke with a start. "What is it?" she asked groggily.

He pulled her from the bed. "The hotel's on fire."

TWENTY

Lila looked at him in shock, standing dressed in his flannel shirt in his bedroom.

"What?"

"The hotel's on fire." Spur took her hand. "We have to leave. Now!"

Lila allowed Spur to lead her into the hall. Thick smoke filled the air.

"Fire! Fire!" a man yelled, banging on doors as he moved through the smoke-shrouded hall.

"Let's try the stairs," Spur said. They moved through the passage, coughing and bumping into dazed men in various states of undress. The smoke was so thick that Spur had to grope along the wall until he found the staircase.

Lila began to step onto it, but Spur pulled her back. Flames lapped at the bottom and inched their way up, eating the runner and jumping a step at a time.

Lila screamed and Spur held her back, then took her into the hall again.

"There's no back stairs," Lila said, then coughed.

"Then it'll have to be a window."

"But we're on the second floor!" she said.

"That doesn't matter. It's better than being smoked to death. Come on, Lila!"

He pulled her harshly toward him and they made their way through the bustling men and smoke toward the window at the hall's end. Fortunately the fire must have been set on the ground floor, leaving most of the hotel's population time to escape. Whoever lived on the first floor, though. . . .

Spur's thoughts raced. Julie. Was she alive? Had she been killed in her sleep? He shook the thoughts off; time enough for that later. He had to get Lila out first before he looked for Julie.

They reached the window and found several men trying to exit through it at once. A fist fight broke out and a man's nose was bloodied, then his opponent leaped through the window. A scream followed soon. Spur craned his neck and saw that the man had impaled himself on a street sign ten feet below.

"Not that way. We'll use the window in my room."

But Spur," Lila said, shaking. "I'm afraid of heights."

"Come on anyway!"

The heat intensified, as did the roar of the flames that burned below them. He turned to see Lila stumbling; her eyes were nearly shut and her lower lip hung lifelessly.

He slapped her cheek hard. It brought her around and before she could respond verbally Spur pulled her with him. If she wouldn't go out the window maybe there was another way. Lila coughed continuously from the smoke, and once nearly fainted, so Spur picked her up, carried her to the stairs, and looked down them.

The fire had gone out before it had risen far up the stairs. They still looked sound. Beyond them the floor was aflame in several spots, but was still intact, from what he could see by the light of the flames that lapped the walls, and in the dim sunlight that filtered in through the smoke.

Spur picked his way down the stairs, carrying Lila tightly in his arms, jumped over the burning steps at the foot and made it halfway to the door.

Lila looked at him; she was fully conscious again, so he let her down onto her feet. The heat was more intense than it had been before and Spur saw why.

One wall was a mass of flames and the fire was still spreading, eating up the timber and furnishings with astonishing vigor.

The front door was ten feet from them. They ran to it and Spur reached for the knob. The brass singed his hand so he let go, backed and slammed his boot against the wood. He repeated the motion a second time and the door opened open. Lila rushed out and Spur followed, then remembered Julie. He turned to Lila.

"Julie might still be in there. I have to find her."

"You saw how the flames were spreading!" she said, grasping his arm.

"I have to see." He wrenched his arm free of Lila's hand and made his way back into the inferno. In his absence the fire had grown; all four walls were aflame. Cinders and burning particles of wallpaper and cloth drifted through the air and smoke hung everywhere. The door to Julie's room stood open. Spur ran to it and stared inside as a burst of light erupted; the draperies on the window had ignited. In their glow his eyes searched the bedroom. She wasn't there.

Spur turned to leave. She must be outside. Sweat poured from his body as he ran for the door. A huge beam crashed down before him and he heard the ceiling groan. Spur darted around the wood and shot out the front door just as the ceiling collapsed.

Julie and Lila stood together twenty feet from the fire.

"I found her," Lila said.

Both women's faces were black with soot and smoke. Julie and Lila stood holding each other, coughing and watching the fire with horrified eyes.

"Glad you made it out," Spur said to Julie.

"Sorry you had to look for me."

Lila hesitated, then put her hand out. Spur put his arms around both women and together they watched the flames consume the building, knowing the bucket brigade that had started was useless. They moved farther back as the flames increased in height and the building crumbled. As Spur turned to look at Julie he saw the flames reflected in her tears.

After a cup of whiskey in Lila's room, Spur glanced to where she lay in her bed sleeping. He turned the lamp down to a dim glow and quietly left.

"How is she?" Julie said, rising from her chair in the hall. Her hair was disarrayed and her face still showed signs of the smoke.

"Fine. She's sleeping. How are you?"

"Okay. I'll stay here for the rest of the morning at least. Why?"

"I have something to do. If anything happens, yell. Someone'll come to help you."

She nodded.

Spur paused, took his Winchester from his back, and made sure it was loaded. Julie stared at the weapon, then shivered. He looked at her. He hadn't mentioned it yet, and it seemed to him that she had avoided the subject as well. Finally he spoke.

"I'm sorry, Julie."

She looked at him in surprise, and Spur knew she hadn't read his thoughts.

"Sorry? About what?"

"Your hotel. I'm responsible."

She shook her head. "No. You're responsible for nothing! You didn't know the raiders would set fire to the hotel."

"I shouldn't have taken her there."

"They could've burned it up anyway, on the chance that you had."

"You don't know that," Spur said, catching her gaze. He slung his rifle back over his shoulder.

"Spur McCoy, you're the stubbornnest man I've ever met. Don't worry. One of the things my father taught me before he died is to be prepared. I got some of this new insurance they started up. A man came by from Denver last month. You pay them money and they take the risk against damage to your place. Lots of farmers have it. With luck it'll pay for the hotel and I can start all over." She sighed. "Now go do what you have to do. I'll watch Lila."

Spur bent and kissed her cheek, then exited the boarding house. Smoke still scented the air outside; he turned and saw the black heap of rubble where the hotel had stood, then untied his horse and rode out of town as the clouds broke and sunlight spilled along the land before him.

When he reached the raiders' camp he found what he'd expected—nothing. The remains of the camp-fire had been carefully covered over; even the footprints had been smoothed out of the dirt, leaving only anonymous horseshoe impressions on the earth. There was nothing to show that hours before the place had been the scene of Lila's rape by the raiders.

Spur realized now what had happened, or thought he did. Johnson had let him and Lila go, then had sent out some men to follow them and set fire to the Wyler Hotel, hoping to kill them both inside. It was a sloppy move.

Spur was certain that Johnson wanted him dead, and the hotel fire was probably the easiest way to do it, although it was also the least sure method.

Rontrell . . . Clint Johnson. They had to be one and the same man, but Spur had no evidence. If he did, he might take it to the sheriff and have him decide what to do. But he couldn't. Sheriff McCormick might believe him and lock up Johnson, which could be the cleanest way to end the raiders' reign of terror. But Spur couldn't take the risk that McCormick might refuse to act on the matter, then alert Rontrell to Spur's suspicions.

No. All he could do was follow Johnson day and night until he left for another meeting with the raiders, then kill as many of them as he could. He had to kill Johnson. Even if Johnson were the only man he did kill, the raiders would, in all probability, scatter and never regroup.

From all evidence, Johnson had organized and trained his raiders. He was their leader, their reason for existing as a group. He paid them, gave them assignments. Without Johnson the raiders would have no leader, no causes, no organization.

Spur decided he'd chance attending the next raiders' meeting alone, with no armed help. He couldn't ride up to the fire with half a dozen men and expect to surprise Johnson. He had to have that advantage—surprise—if he expected to kill the man.

He gently touched his spurs to the horse's sleek flanks. She snorted once, looked at him, then followed his command by galloping back to Fargo.

Kill Johnson—that was his concern now. Kill Johnson and the raiders would cease to be. His assignment would be over.

Before returning to Lila's boarding house, Spur rode down Elm Street. He slowed as he passed the impressive Johnson house, with its shimmering paint and carefully tended grounds. The windows caught the early morning sunlight and blinded him momentarily.

Spur blinked and rode on.

TWENTY-ONE

Spur stood before Lila's room, blocking the door, while she slept inside, recovering from the raiders' assaults. He rolled and lit a cigarette, then puffed while he waited for Julie's return. He hoped she'd have good news.

In the three hours that had passed since the fire, Spur had learned there had been only one fatality connected with the blaze, the man who'd jumped from the window. Many of the guests in Julie's hotel had previously lodged at the Drake and Mason, so they had immediately left the hotel when they first smelled smoke.

Spur looked up with a start when he heard footfalls on the stairs. He dropped his cigarette, crushed it out on the wooden floor, and stood ready for action.

Julie bustled in, her cheeks pink with the chilled air outside. She was smiling.

"Good news?" Spur asked.

"I don't know for sure. I talked to the man who sold me the insurance. He's been in town for a month or so now. From what he said I should have a check within a few weeks."

"Great. And then you'll rebuild the hotel?"

She shrugged. "I'm not sure. I may give this up and go back East, or to Denver. I don't know that I belong here, Spur. It's . . . it hasn't felt like home since Daddy died."

"I'm sorry to hear that, Julie."

"That, and the raiders. . . ." She shivered. "I don't want to worry about them any more."

"I don't think you'll worry much longer."

She looked at him in wonder. "What makes you say that? They seem to be stronger than ever. Spur McCoy, do you know something you're not telling me?"

He smiled. "Guessing, just guessing. I think Rontrell has played his little game long enough. He'll tire of it and move somewhere else—or the law will catch up with him."

Julie smiled. "So you *don't* know. I thought maybe you did, that you'd seen the sheriff or something. Maybe what's happened is all for the best; I could go back to Philadelphia and see my aunt and uncle. Maybe I could open up a new business there—a dress shop, for instance."

"You sew your own clothing?"

"Every stitch I wear." She blushed and giggled. "And I do some sewing for some of the other women here, in exchange for goods."

"I see. That's a beautiful dress you're wearing.

With that talent you could make a small fortune."

"Why, just this morning Clint Johnson commented on my dress; it's a new one."

The name hit Spur like a thunderbolt. "Clint Johnson?"

"Yes. I saw him on the street."

"Do you know where he was going?"

"To the mayor's, I believe. Why?"

"Nothing. I just remembered I have to see him. You'll be okay here with Lila?"

"Yes, fine." She looked at Spur searchingly. "What's wrong?"

"Nothing. I've got to leave. I don't know when I'll be back, but see that Lila gets everything she needs."

"Should I call the doctor?"

"No," Spur said, with force.

"All right."

"She just needs some rest. Stay with her until I'm back."

He left the boarding house and walked down Main Street to the mayor's office. As he approached it he saw Johnson exit the building. Spur stepped back into the shadow and watched the man leave, then followed him surreptitiously.

Johnson went to the bank next, stayed inside for an hour or more, then visited Kelly's Saloon. Spur felt comfortable and safe in entering the saloon; Johnson wouldn't try anything in public, and never while he wasn't masked.

Spur got a beer and sat at a table in the back, keeping his eyes lowered but occasionally glancing at Rontrell. The wealthy man drank and spoke with someone, seemingly oblivious to Spur's presence.

Sheriff McCormick came in and sat at Spur's table and smiled.

"McCoy, I need to talk with you."

"What about?"

"Rontrell."

Spur shrugged. "Why me?"

"Because I think you know something about him. I think that's why you're in Fargo, to find out who he is and put an end to the raiders."

"How'd you arrive at that conclusion?" Spur kept his voice low, neutral, betraying no emotion. He was playing a poker game with McCormick, a poker game of words.

"I got to thinking that night, when I had to keep you locked up. I knew you weren't Rontrell, but I couldn't figure out who the hell you were. I've just come to that conclusion. After all, you did get your hotel window shot out; and you were in the hotel when it was set on fire. And everyone knows—at least now they know—how you rode off and rescued Lila from the raiders last night around midnight."

Spur wondered how the news had spread: either from Johnson himself or possibly from Julie, when she was out earlier that morning.

"And?"

"And it seems you've been mixed up with them more than anyone else in town was. Now it seems to me that you're really here to do something about them. I don't know how or why, but that's what it seems to me." McCormick smiled when Spur looked up at him. "Surprised? I thought you would be. You've been keeping it a secret, but there are some things that can't get past me."

"You're wrong."

McCormick's smile faded. "About what?"

"I'm not here to deal with the raiders. Someone in town's got a grudge against me. That's why my window was shot out. And when I saw Lila being kidnapped by the raiders I did what any man would do—I tried to help her."

"You expect me to believe that?" The sheriff tapped his glass on the table. "I have it all figured out."

"I can't tell you what to think, but I can tell you when your thinking's wrong." Spur finished his beer and rose to get another, but McCormick held his arm.

"That's not all I think."

"No?" Spur asked.

"No. Sit a minute, McCoy. Hell, I don't care whether you're working on the raiders or not, or whether that's why you're in Fargo. But I have to talk with you."

"I don't have anything to say to you."

"Yes you do. You can tell me where you found the raiders and Lila Fairley last night."

Spur hadn't expected that. The sheriff wanted to nab Rontrell and needed Spur's help.

"Hell, McCormick, when did you get interested in the raiders? You haven't done a damn thing about them for weeks."

"I haven't had anything to work with. Now you must've followed them last night and found where they were camped out. Chances are they'll be there again the next time they get together. I can have the place watched and when Rontrell shows up there again I can kill him or take him prisoner."

Spur shook his head. "Rontrell wouldn't be that stupid."

"What are you talking about?"

"Do you think he'd assemble his raiders in exactly the same spot where I found them last night? No. He knows I'm alive and he wouldn't dare do it, on the chance that I might tell you the meeting place."

McCormick put his fist under his chin and thought. Finally he said, "Damn if you're not right. Why didn't I think of that?"

"So even if I did tell you where I found them—which I won't—it wouldn't be any use to you."

"I've got to do something, McCoy. And somehow, with everything you know about the raiders, you can help me."

"Let me know if you find a way."

Spur rose again; the sheriff rose with him.

"It's against the law to withhold information about criminals, McCoy. If you deliberately try to block me or withhold information about Rontrell and the raiders I'll have to lock you up."

"I'm not blocking you and you have no proof that I'm any good to you, McCormick. Cut the tough guy act, it doesn't suit you."

"I'll be watching you, McCoy," McCormick said, and sat down at the table.

Spur went to the bar. On the way there he noticed Johnson still sitting in the same place, his back to Spur. After getting another beer and paying, Spur returned to his table, where McCormick sat sullenly staring into his empty glass.

"McCormick, the land around here's so feature-less that I couldn't even tell you where they were last, if I wanted to."

"There are landmarks—rocks and hills, woods and streams."

"Which I don't know, not being a native. All I can tell you is that they rode out of town west. I followed them for twenty or thirty minutes before they turned off the trail."

"Which direction?" McCormick snapped.

"I don't remember; I was in a hurry." Spur knew he had to give the man some information to prevent the threatened incarceration. He hoped what he had said was adequate.

"It's something to work on, at least. Thanks, McCoy. And if you hear anything, be sure to let me know."

"Sure, McCormick."

The tall sheriff stood and wandered toward the bar. As Spur lifted his glass he saw Johnson rise and start for the door. Spur gulped down the beer and followed. One his way out he checked the time: eleven-thirty.

As he watched Johnson, Spur wondered when the man would try again to kill him. The certainty of the idea didn't bother him, but he would like to be prepared for it.

Johnson stopped in the general store. Spur couldn't follow the man in, so he sat opposite the store on a barrel, waiting. Soon afterward Johnson emerged holding two boxes and walked toward Elm Street.

Following, Spur figured that Johnson was returning home. This was confirmed when Johnson went up the steps of the gaudy house and disappeared into it.

Spur was suddenly wracked with the feeling that he was being watched. He swung around and saw a man disappear behind a corner on Main Street. Johnson must be having him followed.

He hurried around the corner but found no one; the man must have ducked into a store or a saloon. At least Spur was alerted; he'd have to be careful. He didn't want Johnson to know that he knew his other identity.

Spur didn't want to watch Johnson's home for several hours, waiting for the man to emerge, but he knew there was no other way. He found that he could clearly see the front door of Johnson's home from Main Street, and there was a bench placed conveniently beside the wall of Finney's Hotel. He sat and rolled a smoke but didn't light it. While watching Johnson's home he fingered the cigarette until the glue failed and tobacco spilled out onto the ground beneath him.

As he had expected, Johnson didn't budge from his home. Spur felt hunger knot his stomach but he didn't want to move from his vantage point even for food.

Ten minutes later he felt a tap on his shoulder and saw Lila Fairley standing before him, holding a wicker hamper.

"What are you doing out of bed?" he asked, rising.

"I do leave it once in a while," she said with a twinkle. "I'm fine, there's nothing wrong with me. I was just tired, that's all. I did breathe in some smoke but it didn't kill me."

"And the raiders didn't hurt you?"

She sighed. "I'm a little sore but that never killed anyone. I'll be back in commission in a week or so, I'd say."

"I still think you should be in bed," Spur said. "And I don't think it's safe for you to be on the streets."

"Honestly, Spur, you sound like my mother did when I was a little girl. I'm fine and perfectly safe. Anyway, I went for a walk and saw you out here, just sitting, so I figured you were watching somebody or something, like we did before. I also figured you hadn't had anything to eat and I managed to get some food together for you."

She handed him the hamper and sat on the bench, then motioned for him to do the same. She searched the surrounding area, then looked at Clint Johnson's home.

"That it? That's what you're watching, isn't it?"

"I don't want to talk about it," Spur said. "I'm just sitting here resting." He opened the hamper and pulled away the folds of cloth to find fried chicken, a hunk of cheese, three slices of bread, two apples and a bottle of beer.

"Thanks, Lila," he said, his stomach growling.

"Hope it's enough."

Spur ate quickly while Lila watched in amusement.

"You don't have regular meals, do you? Spur, I'm

surprised you're as healthy as you are, missing sleep every other night, never eating."

"Now you sound like *my* mother," Spur said, before washing the cheese down with a swallow of beer. He didn't bother using the glass Lila had provided.

She laughed and sat back on the bench, waiting until he was finished.

When Spur was through she took the hamper, along with the empty bottle, and stood.

"I don't suppose you'd care to walk me back to my room, would you? I mean, to protect me." Lila smiled wickedly.

"No. I think you'll be safe enough. But be careful."

"Don't worry, Spur." She slipped her purse off her shoulder and opened it, then pulled out a wicked-looking derringer.

"That's fine. Do you know how to shoot it?"

"Of course," she said.

"Don't keep it there, in your purse. If you needed it you never get to it in time."

She thought for a minute, then looked at him in frustration. "But where can I keep it? I won't wear a holster and it's too big to go down the front of my dress."

"I'm sure you'll think of something," Spur said with a smile.

Lila pursed her lips momentarily, then shrugged. "Thanks for the advice, Spur. Have a good rest."

She walked off, leaving him with a full belly and less concern for her safety. He wondered why she hadn't used the derringer last night when Rontrell

180

grabbed her, and decided she hadn't had the time, or that she hadn't had her purse with her.

TWENTY-TWO

Clint Johnson paced in his study, watching the flames that he had kindled in the fireplace. When they were high enough, and the dried wood was snapping and smoking, he took the pile of papers he'd stacked on his desk and threw them, two at a time, onto the blaze. The paper caught quickly and within three minutes every sheet was destroyed. Johnson backed from the fire, wiped sweat from his brow and frowned.

He shouldn't have to do this, and he wouldn't have had to if the fire had killed Spur at the Wyler Hotel. Johnson was sure he was doing the right thing, that destroying the papers he'd kept on the raiders—the accounts of raids, the personnel involved, the frequency of meetings and business discussed—was expedient, and ensured that they would not fall into the wrong hands. But it still seemed a waste—insurance he wished he'd never had to pay.

But he had written the records with the knowledge that they might become too dangerous to possess; he had even kept them in his wall safe hidden behind a painting. Until Spur was dead he could take no chances.

Johnson had decided to lay low; whether Spur knew his real identity or not was unknown to him, but it warranted some thought. He hadn't heard a hint of it, so Spur wasn't making public the accusation that Johnson and Rontrell were one and the same, and for that Johnson was glad.

But something about Spur's conduct at the camp last night had made Johnson suspicious that Spur knew who he was. That, as well as the fact that Spur had taken Lila from the raiders and had killed two of them, was good cause to have the hotel burned. But he shouldn't have taken that course, he saw now; he should have had Spur and the girl killed quickly then and there.

That was in the past, though; he turned his thoughts to the future. He could wait a few days; Spur would be hard to touch, on his guard. Johnson was certain that Spur would be expecting something from him. He'd make the man wait.

At the best moment, when Spur was in the best place and time, he would kill Spur and be done with him forever.

But there were other plans to be made—the raiders needed a new meeting site. Johnson realized that Spur would watch the other place, so that was out. But the site had been perfect and would be hard to replace.

For a moment he toyed with the idea of meeting at his house, but the same disadvantages applied—too many people might notice the men gathering there, and whatever excuse he gave might not be believed. No, too risky; he'd have to choose somewhere else.

The Flint Hills were too far for short meetings and most of the rest of the territory was unsuitable, with little cover from prying eyes. He sighed and drummed his fingers on the desk.

There was the place near Judson's Creek; it was surrounded by trees and wasn't more than twenty-five minutes from town, well off the trail west. The trees provided little shielding, so they couldn't build a fire, but they could survive that—at least until Spur was dead. It would do nicely.

Still, no matter how secluded their spot was, Johnson had to consider the possibility that Spur would find them and cause trouble. If that was the case, Johnson had to be ready for him—especially if Spur didn't come alone, but with the sheriff and perhaps a posse.

He had to ensure that he could escape and stay out of Fargo for several days, possibly in the hills. It shouldn't be too hard to lose himself for a few days out there. Then he could either go back to Fargo or go on to Denver—a long train ride but perhaps a necessary one.

Another precaution: he'd have his saddlebags filled with enough provisions to last him a week or more, as well as several full canteens. The only problem might be the weather, but he couldn't control that.

Johnson smiled indulgently and rubbed his hands. Even if Spur did show up at a meeting and started causing trouble, he'd be gone before the man knew it!

There was a curt knock on the door, then it opened. He looked up. "What do you want, Francine?"

The woman was plump, tall and richly dressed. She moved toward him with an air of unmistakeable elegance.

"Money," she said, her fleshy chin rippling as she said the word. "Money, jewels, power—keep it simple."

"Spare me your humor, Francine."

"I do need some money. The new drapes for the parlor have arrived and I need to pay for them."

"Don't you have any of your own money? What happens to the five hundred I give you every month?"

"It evaporates," she said coolly. "Like pearls in wine."

He laughed shortly, moved to the wall facing the fireplace and removed the painting, revealing the wall safe. He swiftly dialed the combination and the door swung open smoothly. Johnson removed several stacks of bills and bags of coins.

"How much do you need this time?"

"Fifty."

He got the money, handed it to her, and closed the safe. After scrambling the tumblers and replacing the painting, he smiled at his sister.

"Is that all? I'm busy."

She looked at his clean desk and smirked.

"No. I want you to do something about Spur McCoy."

"I'm doing everything I can," he said quietly.

She shook her head and regarded him harshly. "Not enough. He's too close to us. I feel his hot breath down the back of my dress. If you don't do something, Clint, I will. I'm not going to let one man jeopardize all your plans!" Her eyes were steely grey.

"Neither am I," he said angrily. "Do you think I'm frightened of him? Of course not. The man's a fool. But I have to wait until I can get near him. I don't want to kill him on the street in the middle of the day; that would be suitable, but it's too risky at this stage. Fargo is ready to rebel; with my luck, whoever killed Spur would be captured and tortured until he talked. That development would put you and me out of reach of our money for several years."

"They wouldn't dare throw a woman in prison!" she said.

"Perhaps not. Maybe they'd hang you."

She looked at him sharply. "No."

"I didn't ask you to get involved in this affair, Francine," Johnson said. "When you discovered it I had no choice but to bring you into it. But I won't have you trying to run my operation! The raiders are mine."

"True. All right, I see your point. Go slow on Spur, but get rid of him. We're not finished in Fargo yet; there's still work to be done."

"I know, Francine; I know." Clint sighed and watched his sister exit his study.

The woman was driving him to the brink, but she was right, damnit. She was always right. Johnson sat and propped his feet on his desk, folded his hands and laid them over his stomach, and sighed again.

Things were not going well.

At three o'clock Mayor Zane Evans appeared in Johnson's study.

"I'm here as ordered, Mr. Johnson. What did you want to see me about?"

Johnson frowned and leaned against the mantel. "We've having a meeting tonight. Everyone. It's very important."

"I—I see. Do you think that's such a good idea so soon after Spur—"

"It's not your place to dictate my actions!" Johnson thundered.

"I know, but—"

"Shut up and listen. I'm moving the meeting site. The other one's no good; Spur knows its location. I've decided to relocate to that old oak grove near Judson's Creek. You know, the place where they were going to cut for timber until they found out most of the trees weren't sound?"

Evans, red faced, nodded.

"Good. Inform everyone—and I do mean everyone—of the new meeting site. Be as discreet as possible. Make it for seven P.M. Have you got that?"

Evans nodded. "Yes, Mr. Johnson."

"Then get your ass out of my study!" he said.

The frightened mayor bobbed his head again, then slipped through the door and was gone.

Johnson glared at the door. Evans wasn't worth much as a mayor, but he made a hell of a good pawn.

TWENTY-THREE

At sundown, Spur stood and stretched. The bench had grown hard and uncomfortable during his five hours on it, and he was restless for action.

Johnson hadn't left his home since he'd entered it, and Spur hadn't expected him to. Not until after dark. Then, if luck were with him, Johnson would ride off to a meeting of his raiders, and Spur could kill or wound the man and put the group out of commission.

The thought warmed his gut, and he sat and rolled a cigarette, glancing from the gaudy house only briefly, at intervals. Johnson must be stewing inside, mapping out a way to exterminate Spur. He smiled at the idea, then frowned. It wouldn't be so easy to follow Johnson or his men to the meeting, if he had the opportunity again. Johnson would be more watchful; he'd have to use different tactics.

He sat back on the hard wooden bench and puffed

189

at his smoke, glancing again at the imposing structure on the corner, five hundred feet from him.

The front door opened and Clint Johnson appeared on the porch. Spur didn't rise, but he readied himself to move fast. Johnson paced on the porch, hands clasped against the small of his back. What was the man waiting for?

Spur heard a horse approaching behind him; it passed and continued to Johnson's home, then halted. The rider, whom Spur recognized as Mayor Zane Evans, dismounted and met Johnson halfway up the steps that led to the porch.

They engaged in animated conversation; Spur wished he could hear the words, but the distance was too great. A minute later Evans rode off and Johnson disappeared again within his home.

Spur had seen the mayor visit Johnson earlier that day, but hadn't thought much about it. Politics and money always mix, even in small towns. But the mayor's second visit signaled more than political maneuvering.

The conclusion was obvious. His supicions concerning Evans were correct—the mayor was a raider. He had no proof, but needed none.

So the richest man in town and the mayor were involved in the raids. Who else? The sheriff? The judge? Everyone with power or influence?

It wouldn't be the first time, but Spur doubted it. Johnson had some kind of hold over his raiders; if it wasn't blackmail, it was either money or anger. He was either paying them for their efforts, or channeling their anger, or both.

That he gave them an outlet for their anger

provided him with control over the raiders. It had happened before, and Spur was sure that was the case here.

He mulled over the idea as dusk deepened into night, and a cold moon hung like a pale lemon just above the flat eastern horizon.

At sixt-thirty Johnson left his home, dressed in jeans and a flannel shirt—just as Spur had seen him at the firelit raiders' meetings. Good. He hadn't been wrong. Johnson was Rontrell.

The man climbed onto his horse and rode at a leisurely trot. Spur had no trouble walking to his horse, mounting it and locating Johnson again; but to his surprise the man moved west.

Johnson was no fool; he wouldn't have his men meet in the same location. Or would he?

Spur realized as soon as they were out of Fargo that the night was too dark to follow Johnson at a great distance. If he'd had time he would have tied cloth around his horse's hooves to deaden their noise, but that was impossible now; he couldn't stop, and he had no rags to use.

Perhaps Johnson would mistake him for one of his raiders, Spur stayed as far back as he could, but never more than a hundred yards behind Johnson. Farther away, he would lose sight of the man.

Spur stayed his horse several times, bringing her behind trees or into the brush. Twice he jumped to the ground when he thought Johnson would glance behind him, but apparently the man hadn't seen him. After ten minutes Johnson increased his speed and caught Spur off guard. For a moment the raider disappeared into the darkness in front of Spur.

He gently pushed his horse faster, unwilling to speed too much and find himself at the barrel end of Johnson's rifle, but knowing he had to pick up the man again.

Finally he saw a moving blur several hundred feet before him. Johnson. Good. Spur decreased the distance between himself and the other man, but still kept back.

When they passed the signal tree, where the red handkerchief had hung, Spur knew that Johnson wasn't using the old site. Instead of turning south and heading for the cliff-shrouded spot, Johnson continued due west.

He was surprised that the sheriff had thought Johnson would return to the same place. The lawman wasn't too bright, or he was just plain careless in his thinking.

It was then that Spur heard a noise behind him, the soft neigh of a horse. Spur spotted a low stand of trees ahead, dense enough in the dim moonlight to conceal him and his mount. He rode for those trees. Once among the thin, sheltering trunks of the elms, he watched the road.

Several riders, all masked, passed by the wood where he sat watching. The raiders were going to the meeting place. Spur checked the urge to open fire on them; surprise was an advantage, but it had to be surprise in a controlled situation. On the road the men could scatter; grouped around a fire they were easier and slower moving targets.

Thirteen men passed him, some coming so close he could see the patterns on the handkerchief masks.

His bay stirred, but Spur placed a hand over the muzzle to keep her from neighing.

When no man had passed him for several minutes, Spur decided it was safe and rode down the faint trail again. If a raider did come upon him, he could assume Spur was one of them, in the darkness.

For some reason Spur had thought Johnson would be the last man to the meeting but apparently the reverse was true. He followed the dark mass of riders that made up the raiders, ignoring the cold that battered down on him. Fortunately it had been chilly all day and he'd never removed his coat after he'd retrieved it from Lila.

He heard it again—the whinnying of a horse behind him, breaking the stillness of the night. Spur saw no cover nearby, so he continued to ride, but pulled a handkerchief from his pocket and tied it around his head to cover his nose and mouth. If he did meet up with the raider he hoped it was one who didn't know the identities of all his fellows.

Surprisingly, he met no one and could see no rider behind him. Either the rider had a slow mount or the wind had tricked Spur's ears.

He glanced at the raiders and saw that they had left the trail and were headed north. He gazed at the Flint Hills; moonlight played along the low, rolling mountains that, for all their lack of height, were impressive in the relatively flat, monotonous Kansas surroundings.

Spur didn't cut across the land but continued along the trail until he came to the spot where he believed the raiders broke from it, and followed them. In the distance, seemingly near the foot of the hills, he saw a densely wooded patch and surmised that that was the raiders' destination.

Johnson must be there already, but Spur saw no signs of a fire. Perhaps Johnson had even dispensed with that, in light of the events of the last few days.

Soon the men disappeared into the black patch of oaks and Spur knew he had been right. The trees provided little cover, up close. They were spaced well apart, though the thin moonlight barely penetrated them, so from a distance the whole area seemed black as soot. Spur also realized that there was little cover for him to use to watch the raiders as well; he'd have to be cautious.

He tied up his horse at the edge of the trees and moved silently until he neared the center of the copse. There in a natural clearing Clint Johnson hung a lantern from the branch of a tree and struck a match. Moments later a thin light penetrated the darkness and illuminated the area softly.

The raiders were there, grouped around Johnson in a semicircle. They sat without talking and Johnson planted his hands on his hips as he looked over his men.

Spur quietly moved five feet closer to the raiders and stopped, half crouching behind a broad-trunked oak. As he gazed at Rontrell and his men, a bone-dry, golden-brown leaf fell from above him and landed on the ground.

Rontrell finally spoke. "You and you, do guard duty but stay close by. I don't expect any trouble but we can't be sure. Report back to me every hour; otherwise stay quiet and still."

The men he'd pointed to nodded, stood and strode

out of the clearing in opposite directions. One, a short, greasy-looking man in his fifties, sniffed as he passed within ten feet of Spur. The other was safely on the other side of the woods, over a hundred yards from him. All he had to do was get rid of the guard and he had an hour of safe time.

The guard stopped sniffing and leaned against a tree, fiddling with his gun. Spur saw a beam of moonlight glisten along its shaft. He needed a diversion. Looking down at his feet, he saw a plentiful store of acorns lying scattered around the base of the trees. He picked up a good handful and propelled one to land three feet in front of the guard.

With the soft crunch of the acorn hitting the ground, the guard looked up, alert, his finger ready at the trigger. Spur threw more and the guard frowned, then took a step forward. He opened his mouth, then closed it, apparently in memory of Johnson's order to remain silent. But he took three steps, bending his torso slightly forward, peering into the darkness at the maze of tree trunks and heaps of gray leaves.

Spur volleyed three more acorns in rapid succession, then threw more to land by the guard's side. When they landed the man turned sharply to his right and Spur moved up smoothly, removing the blade he kept on his belt. An instant later he had clapped a hand over the man's mouth and plunged the knife between his shoulderblades.

The guard struggled for a moment. The blade lodged firmly in the flesh, Spur grabbed the gun from the man's hand before it could drop to the ground, then laid him down. Moments later the man was dead.

Spur glanced over at the raiders; no one was alerted to the guard's death. He surveyed the area and mapped out his course of action. There was no suitable cover in the trees, nothing substantial save thin trunks, so he couldn't hope to find a strategic point and fight off all fifteen men alone in a drawn-out battle. No, he had to move quickly and hope that surprise would give him time to kill six or seven of them and the others would flee from the scene.

He had to have his mount beside him in order to ride away hard and fast if the men stood their ground and returned fire. Spur moved silently through the trees, reached his horse at the edge of the woods, and had turned to lead it back with him when he heard a sound behind him. He spun around and saw a man standing there. As he drew he realized with a start that the man was Sheriff Mc-Cormick.

TWENTY-FOUR

"What the hell are you doing here?" Spur's voice was barely a whisper, but the sheriff heard it as they confronted each other at the edge of the trees that hid the raiders' camp.

"Same reason you're here," the sheriff said, moving closer to Spur.

"Keep your voice down," Spur said.

"Sure."

"How'd you find the place?"

"I followed you." Spur saw his teeth gleam yellowly in the moonlight.

"You come alone?"

"Yes. I didn't want to risk bringing anyone with me. The more men with you, the more chance you'll be found out. No, I'm alone. And I'm going to take care of Rontrell."

"You're not going to do anything," Spur said, "except ride back to Fargo and forget about this."

"You must be crazy. What is it, Spur—you want all the glory for killing Rontrell?"

Spur shook his head. "I work alone. Understand? You'll fuck up my plans. Get the hell out of here, McCormick."

"I'm the law here. You can't tell me what to do."

"All right. You tell me how you're going to take care of Rontrell and his twelve armed men."

McCormick hesitated. "I hadn't thought about that yet. Hell, I didn't even know for sure if this was where you were going. I guess I'll ride back to town, gather up a posse, and have at it with them."

Spur shook his head. "That'll take you nearly an hour, and by that time they'll be gone from here. No, McCormick, it won't work."

"What's your plan?"

"I don't have to tell you that."

"Humor me," the sheriff said.

"To kill Rontrell."

"I see."

"I figure if they lose their leader, the raiders will scatter and never regroup. Even if I don't kill them all or put them behind bars, at least the raiders as a unit will have been dispersed and the threat to Fargo will be gone."

McCormick shook his head. "Makes sense. But maybe it's time you leveled with me. It's obvious to me and half the town by now that you came to Fargo because of the raiders. Why?"

Spur hesitated, then sighed. He couldn't say anything. "Get the hell out of here, McCormick. I don't want you in my way when I start shooting."

The sheriff frowned. "Damn you, Spur," he

growled, "you can't do this alone! You're right about the posse—the raiders might be gone by the time I came back with them. Why don't you let me help you clean them up?"

Spur shrugged. "I don't want you here." He checked his Colt .44 to see that it was loaded and ready to be used, ignoring the sheriff's reaction. The man's sudden appearance had upset Spur's plans. If he couldn't talk the sheriff into leaving he'd have to rethink his strategy.

Whatever he did, it couldn't make much noise. He realized that if he lost his surprise he'd have little chance of killing Rontrell and half his men, as he'd hoped. But maybe, if he could get the sheriff to cooperate, he would be a help.

He looked at the sheriff and smiled. "All right, McCormick," he whispered. "You can help me. We'll move as close to the raiders as we can, hiding behind trees. I'll fire the first shot; it'll be directed at Johnson. Don't fire until you hear me. Got that?"

McCormick nodded, then went white in the moonlight. "Johnson? Clint Johnson? You mean he's out there?"

Spur nodded. "He's Rontrell. I thought you knew."

The sheriff shook his head. "No, I hadn't even considered the possibility. I've known him for—two years? Three? Surely you're mistaken, McCoy."

"I'm not. I followed him here. He *is* Rontrell."

"I see."

The man was despondent.

"Don't back out on me now, McCormick! You wanted to help me? Fine, help me! Shoot into them after I start. But wait for me! You got that?"

"Sure," the sheriff said.

"Come on. Let's move our horses in so we can ride out fast if we have to."

The sheriff did so, following Spur stealthily into the woods, nearing the clearing and the dim glow of the lantern. As they moved closer Spur heard Clint Johnson's voice.

"Any questions?" it asked.

"Sure. What about Lila Fairley?" another man said.

"We'll see. I don't know; she hasn't done us any harm . . . yet. But I want you boys to go easy on her. She knows she can't refuse any of us if we want to bed her—but she's the type who might do something stupid, like turning one of us in. So be careful, but firm, with her. As soon as Spur's out of our hair—which will be soon, I assure you—we'll take care of McCormick and Fargo will be ours!"

Spur heard McCormick move beside him.

"Jesus," he said.

"That's your friend there," Spur said in a sardonic whisper. McCormick began to reply, but Spur waved him silent; they were too close for conversation.

Spur positioned himself behind a tree trunk two feet from where the dead guard lay. As he glanced at the man he saw that the falling leaves had nearly covered him. That was good, in case one of the raiders decided to go for a walk.

Johnson's voice continued, answering questions, while Spur waited, relaxing. The meeting seemed to be nearing its conclusion. The time was right.

He nodded to the sheriff as he stood next to his mount, and aimed. Johnson was thirty feet from him, with only two trees between them. If he took careful aim and Johnson didn't move he should hit him.

Spur looked at McCormick. The man had his Smith & Wesson .44 in a shaky grip, but the hand firmed up when the sheriff saw Spur's glance. The Secret Service man returned his attention to Johnson and had prepared to fire when the raider suddenly moved to his right.

At that moment McCormick's S&W blasted off a shot. Spur took hasty aim at Johnson and fired six times as fast as he could, cursing McCormick.

The raiders jumped to their feet, reaching for their weapons. McCormick cursed beside him. Spur glanced at him as he reloaded, aimed and fired again. McCormick mounted and amid a storm of slugs was gone from sight.

The raiders hustled for cover behind trees; Spur fired until his cylinder was empty, then reloaded. Three men had fallen. As he finished he noticed that Johnson was not among the downed men. A volley of shots rushed past him. The raiders were shooting blind.

He ran a dozen feet to one side and fired once again, but had no target. The returning slugs slowed in frequency until Spur was sure there was only one man shooting at him. He glanced around the tree; the sound of hooves punctuated the air. The raiders, as expected, had fled.

Spur rose, dodged a slug, and slowly circled through the the woods, watching for the last man firing at him. He spotted him and picked him off with one shot, then looked to his right.

Johnson was running to his horse thirty-five feet away. In the filtered moonlight and lantern's glow Spur made positive identification; it was definitely Clint Johnson.

He fired, missed, fired again. Johnson effortlessly lifted himself onto the saddle and in seconds had spurred the animal to a racing gallop through the trees.

Cursing, Spur went to his horse, mounted and guided it through the oaks, searching for Johnson. When he broke from the woods he saw the horse speeding away from him.

Johnson wasn't heading for Fargo, Spur realized with a start. Before him loomed the Flint Hills. The Secret Service man splashed through a silvery stream that must have its origins in the hills, then rode over the open country for which the area was famous.

At that distance Spur had no chance of hitting Johnson. He raced his bay, spurring her gently, wondering why he hadn't packed any provisions on his horse, and whether his canteen were empty.

TWENTY-FIVE

Spur halted his horse momentarily on a low rise at the foot of the Flint Hills. Moonlight made the gentle hills a maze of angles and planes sprinkled with inky shadows.

He looked at the trail of hoofprints he could barely make out below him. If he didn't run into hard earth it shouldn't be difficult to follow Johnson. He'd left in a hurry when Spur surprised his nighttime raider meeting with a volley of shots, but had left clear tracks.

To Spur's surprise Johnson's horse had outrun his, and now the man was somewhere in the hills, hiding out or riding hard, knowing Spur McCoy would follow. He spurred his horse gently; it responded and they dashed toward the blue-gray peaks, following Johnson's trail.

The moonlight held; few clouds obscured its light, so Spur had no trouble following the prints. But despite his mad dash for his bay when he saw

Johnson mount, he hadn't seen the man since he'd ridden from the lanternlit grove after the raiders had scattered.

Johnson had acted so quickly he might have known Spur would be there; perhaps he'd made plans in case that happened. If so, the man was probably well supplied with provisions and could survive several days in the hills.

Spur knew from talk around town, and from his last visit to Fargo, that there were few people living in the hills. There was one ranch, but he had no idea of its location. The gentle mountains, interlaced with rivers, had yet to be fully settled.

Though he expected to find Johnson soon, he had to consider the possibility of spending several days up there. Water was no problem; it flowed around him every mile or so. But food—he'd have to hunt if he wanted to eat.

Spur strained his eyes into the darkness to discern a moving figure, but couldn't see Johnson. The man was taking a direct route to his destination, wasting no time. As they climbed the first hill Spur noticed that the ground grew harder and left shallower impressions, so he had more difficulty following the horse's prints.

He cursed as the prints disappeared. Spur halted his bay and swung down from the saddle, then began a thorough search of the area. The bluish-white moonlight hindered more than helped him now; it tended to gloss over any distinctions in the ground. But after a five-minute delay he found the trail again and mounted. Johnson had veered right, probably to save riding up the face of the slope.

An hour later Spur slowed his horse. It needed the rest; its nostrils blew steam in rhythmic intervals into the chilly night air.

He'd reached the shoulder of the hill and stared out onto the vast panorama of hills and mountains. He thought it looked like a length of blue cloth that had been laid on a flat surface and bunched, creating an endless series of rises and valleys.

Johnson could be hiding in any one of them. If Spur lost the trail he could search for days or weeks and never find the man. He coaxed his horse to a trot down the face of the hill.

The land was remarkably similar to the rest of the Kansas landscape; trees were few but, where present, usually grew along the banks of rivers, which sparkled like ribbons of molten silver.

He passed maples and huge old walnuts, some of which had five-foot-thick trunks. Clumps of wild-flowers, most of which were brown with the onset of winter, studded the ground.

The trail grew lighter as the moon dipped far into the western sky. Spur wasn't worried; moonset should be followed soon after by sunrise.

An eerie rock formation jutted up from the otherwise peaceful series of valleys; when Spur rode near it he was surprised at the sight. Wind and rain had carved it into the perfect image of a woman's profile.

When he had rounded another rise he halted his horse and smelled the air. Smoke, not far away. He peered into the night. Had Johnson stopped and made a fire? The man wouldn't be that stupid, Spur reasoned. But he had no choice—he had to find the fire.

As he continued following the hoofprints, the acrid scent of smoke increased. He recognized the smell—burning oak. If the prints led him to the fire, Spur would soon know if he were right.

Then he saw the faint glow and the column of smoke that stretched skyward not more than five hundred feet from him. The fire had been set beside a narrow river. He slowed his horse. It could be a trap. Johnson wouldn't light a fire, knowing Spur might see it. Or would he? Perhaps he didn't know better.

McCoy approached the fire cautiously. When he was fifty feet from it he halted the bay. No one was in sight. The fire crackled loudly, sending up sparks amid the flames. Green leafy oak branches had been laid over the burning logs to create the excessive amounts of smoke.

Johnson had set the fire deliberately to lure Spur to it, to divert him, or—

Spur sensed the slug whisper past him before he heard the report of the rifle. He dodged his horse behind a massive maple that grew on the banks of the river.

Another shot. Spur unslung his rifle and fired into the brush and trees surrounding the fire, hoping a blind shot would hit Johnson. The explosions echoed through the night. He paused to reload. Silence. Johnson was either dead, gone or waiting.

When the ringing in his ears ceased he heard Johnson's departure. Spur cursed and spurred his horse to a gallop. They broke through the brush and Spur found the hoofprints leading to the river. He waded his horse in; the water wasn't more than a foot deep.

At the other side he couldn't find the trail; the sand was smooth and untouched.

Johnson was smarter than he'd thought. The man had ridden his horse into the stream to cover his tracks. Spur had no idea where he'd left it—upstream or down, to the right or left.

Spur cursed again and held his horse still. It shivered as the water swirled around its legs, but obeyed. He heard the faint sound of splashing to his right, downstream. It could be a waterfall, but it could also be Johnson's horse.

McCoy had spun his bay and started in that direction when he heard a voice cut through the darkness.

"McCoy!"

Johnson? No.

"McCoy, wait!"

Caught between following Johnson's trail and the voice's command, he hesitated. A moment later he saw a rider halt at the edge of the water. Spur walked his bay nearer.

McCormick.

The sheriff's shirt had an ugly dark spot on the side, and he gently swayed in the saddle. His shoulders were stooped. He was wounded.

"McCoy, thank God you heard me."

"What the fuck are you doing here, McCormick?" Spur put more force into his voice than he had intended; the man had ruined his plans earlier and could do so again.

"I have to kill Clint Johnson." The voice was low, devoid of emotion. It was a cold, harsh statement.

Spur led his horse from the water and swung

down, then approached the sheriff. McCormick looked down sullenly at him, then grinned.

"We'll get him. He's close by, ain't he? I lost your trail until I saw this fire and figured you'd be heading here too."

Spur nodded toward the wound. "You get that from Johnson's men at the grove?"

The sheriff nodded and swallowed loudly. "Yeah. Couldn't move fast enough. I started back for town but ran into the raiders. Then I remembered I'd left you back there alone, so . . . I rode back. Got there just in time to see you hightailing it across the creek. Figured you were following someone— Johnson, I guessed—so I decided to help you. After I'd let you down I couldn't forget it. You know." He motioned slightly with his right hand.

The voice was weak. Spur's anger softened into pity; the sheriff was ashamed and had ignored his wound to "help" Spur.

"Look, McCormick, I appreciate the offer, but you're in no condition to ride. Hell, I don't even know how long I'll be out here, checking every valley. You've got to get that hole in your side looked after or you'll be dead in a couple of days.

"Hell," the sheriff said. "I found some whiskey at the raider's camp and splashed some on it. I'm tough. I'm okay."

"You got a slug in there?" Spur asked.

The sheriff nodded.

"That's bad. You can't come with me. I can take care of Johnson alone. Go back to Fargo and get that patched up. I don't blame you for what happened."

"Bullshit!" The sheriff's eyes gleamed in the dark as he spat out the word. An instant later his body trembled and he pitched forward in the saddle. "That's bullshit, McCoy. We both know it." The pain passed. McCormick sat straight. "I fucked up your chance to get a clean shot at Johnson. I'm responsible. Damnit, I'll get Johnson if it's the last thing I do!" McCormick winced, and his left hand automatically went to his side. "Save your breath," he said in a low voice. "I'm going with you."

"Hell, you'll be dead in a day. You can't be too much trouble, I suppose."

Spur didn't want a wounded, groggy, shame-stricken lawman tagging after him, but it seemed he had little choice. He mounted and, ignoring the sheriff, led his bay into the stream and moved down it, toward the direction where he'd heard the suspicious sounds.

McCormick splashed along behind him, occasionally muttering to himself but staying out of Spur's sight. He watched the banks on either side of him, glancing from one to the other, searching for the crescent-shaped indentations in the soft sand that lay piled up to the water's edge. Beyond the banks trees and wildflowers grew in profusion. Spur hoped Rontrell hadn't ridden from the stream, brushed his prints out of the sand, and then hid himself in the bushes. It would be hard for the man to miss Spur with a rifle at such close range.

Ten minutes later Spur saw them. The prints were almost washed away with water, but they were there—deep impressions in the soft sand. The water must have come from the horse's legs as it left the stream.

Spur guided his horse onto the bank and heard a splash behind him. He turned and saw McCormick lying face down in the stream. He jumped from his bay and pulled the man onto the sand. The sheriff mumbled. Spur unbuttoned his shirt and stared at the blood-soaked handkerchief that covered the man's side. He'd lost too much blood to be riding, unless he didn't plan to come back.

McCormick sputtered, coughed, and opened his eyes.

"Spur, I'm finished. Damnit, I'm finished." The man's gaunt, wet face tensed. "I still can't believe it's Johnson." He shook his head sadly and swallowed.

"Don't talk. I'll leave you here, then pick you up and take you to Fargo after I'm through with Johnson. It shouldn't be too long."

"You can't fool me. I've seen too many men die. I've lost a lot of blood. Damnit, McCoy," he said, and then sighed. McCormick didn't draw in another breath.

Spur rose and led the sheriff's horse next to the body and tied it to a branch. He searched around him, glancing at the hills, seeing landmarks so that he could find the place again.

When he'd finished he grimly set out following the tracks again. Spur would pick up the body and horse after he'd killed Johnson.

To his surprise the trail turned sharply to his right and paralleled the river. Johnson mustn't be thinking too well; that made following almost too easy. Then Spur remembered that Johnson could

210

repeat his trick again; he could dip into the river and double back, or go on ahead and get lost in the hills.

Spur sighed and watched the moon set as he followed the tracks. Soon it was too dark for him to move at all; the horse had difficulty picking her way among the rocks and Spur lost all sight of the prints.

He cursed and led the horse to the river, where he tied her next to a still-fresh patch of sweet grass. She drank and then chewed the grass while Spur leaned against a tree trunk, wishing he could build a fire to take the chill off. Instead, he rolled a smoke and lit it, careful to shield the flaring match and then douse it in the river.

His bay looked up, apparently startled by the flame, then calmed and continued munching. The darkness closed around him; the gentle trickle of the river soothed his aching brain, and Spur felt himself edging toward sleep.

He sat up with a start. No time for sleep. Dawn was less than an hour away and he had to be back on the trail by then. He inhaled again, enjoying the harsh tobacco's taste.

If he hadn't been absolutely still, if the night hadn't been quiet, he might have missed the unmistakeable neighing of a horse somewhere out in the blackness around him.

TWENTY-SIX

Spur threw his smoke into the river and stood, straining her ears. Again he heard the shrill cry of the horse.

His bay heard it too, and stood with its head up, ears pricked. It sniffed the air.

The first brushings of dawn crept upward in the east as Spur mounted. He'd have light sooner than expected.

Johnson was nearby. It had to be him, had to be his horse he'd heard. But where was he? The sounds seemed to come from his right. Light was still scarce, with the moon down and the sun not risen yet. Owl time, he remembered an old woman's describing it in a dusty Texas town.

He moved the horse slowly, letting it pick its way through the trees and brush. Spur hoped for another sound from the unseen animal but he knew Johnson would hold its muzzle closed to silence it. He heard nothing more.

The blackness of the sky turned gray. A bird chirped crazily above him. His horse was alert. Spur had no idea where Johnson was. He only knew that he was nearby.

The light increased and Spur saw movement—a rabbit scurried among the trees, saw him, froze, then disappeared seconds later. Spur watched every part of the forest around him, holding his Winchester ready, waiting.

He heard it again. Johnson's horse was not happy. The neighing grew louder, still to his right. Johnson was so close Spur imagined that he could smell the sweat on the man's neck. Then he saw the horse standing, throwing its head back and forth. Three feet from it Johnson stood.

Spur didn't know what was happening between them and he didn't care. He dismounted quietly, moved silently through the trees, halted and lined up Johnson in his sights. The man looked around him, suddenly suspicious.

Just as he saw Spur in the woods aiming, he darted. Spur squeezed off a shot. Johnson's horse bolted and neighed. Spur followed with another round. Johnson screamed and ran for the trees after his horse. Spur moved ahead and saw the man mount his horse.

Surprised, McCoy jumped onto his own saddle and spurred his horse into a flat run. The short rest had refreshed her and she cooperated.

Johnson was less than fifty yards from him. Spur

reloaded as he rode, and fired again. He thought the shot hit home but he didn't know for sure.

Johnson suddenly turned and fired wildly behind him; the slugs flew wide of Spur. The raider repeated the action, then savagely spurred his horse's flanks. The animal poured on more speed and shot away from Spur.

Spur urged his horse faster and watched as Johnson rode out from the strip of trees that grew along the river, onto the rolling land.

He followed, cutting across the woods, and quickly emerged from them, only to find the area before him empty. Johnson was gone.

The sun was nearly up now, the light bright enough for him to scour the area visually. The prints led to a strange ridge of rock formations. He hurried up to it, then thought again and paused before it.

The weird limestone formations, shaped like gortesque figures from a nightmare, stood atop a ridge that must have been a hill before it was eroded by the elements.

It was the perfect place for an ambush. If Spur were Johnson, he would hide behind the ridge, wait for Spur to ride in, then attack.

Spur had to act quickly or Johnson would know that his plan had failed. The ridge was less than five hundred feet high, with the eighty-foot formations standing like sentinels on top. The sides sloped gently in one spot. Spur urged his horse up the relatively flat area.

The animal slowly climbed the slope. Once at the top, Spur dismounted, laid a heavy rock on the reins to ground tie his horse, and crouched behind one of the weird fingers of rock.

He looked around it.

Johnson was huddled behind a patch of brush halfway down the opposite side of the ridge. His horse was nowhere in sight. Spur was too far from the man to make a sure shot. He moved along the top of the ridge, in and out of the rocks, until he was directly above Johnson.

As he knelt to steady himself his knee dislodged a small stone, which rolled down the cliff. It set other pebbles in motion until a dozen rocks crashed down from the ridge.

Johnson looked up. The two men stared at each other and fired. Spur ducked behind the thousand-year-old formation and waited, then moved out from behind it and fired again.

Johnson lay sprawled on the slope behind the bushes. His Smith & Wesson had slid down the ridge.

Spur cautiously made his way down the cliff until he stood beside Johnson. The man's eyes were closed, his face was twisted in pain and his chest rose and fell rapidly.

"Johnson?" Spur asked.

The man opened his eyes.

"Why?" Spur asked. It was a simple question.

The man coughed, sputtering blood. It ran from his lips like a scarlet finger tracing a straight line. "Civil War," he said. "My wife and kids—" Another cough. "Bloody bastards murdered them! Bloody fucking bastards!"

"Who?"

"All of them. Riley. Mason. Drake. All of them.

Yankee raiders, all of them. Outlaws hiding in uniforms. Killed my family, stole our money and burned the house." A tear squeezed from his right eye. "Bloody bastards! I showed them that justice would find them and make them pay! Me and Francine showed them! Then you had to come along. Damn you!"

Spur didn't understand. "You're not making sense."

"Bullshit I'm not!" Johnson said, as a shiver ran through his body. "Goddamn fucking Yankees think they can murder and loot. But I showed them!" The man shook his head. "Until you, McCoy." He closed his eyes and groaned.

Spur looked down; the hole in Johnson's belly was bad. Spur had seen more men die from belly wounds than any other kind.

"Where's your horse?" Spur asked.

"Fuck off!"

"I'll take you back to town."

"So you can murder me? No. That's one thing you can't take from me. I'll do it myself."

Johnson's hand moved swiftly to his belt and unsheathed a six-inch knife. Spur aimed, ready to fire if the man threw it, but was surprised when Johnson gripped the blade and held it to his own heart.

Just as he seemed about to plunge it in between his ribs, Johnson screamed, whipped the blade around, and sent the knife hurling at Spur.

Spur fired his Winchester as the knife fell harmlessly to the hard-packed earth. The slugs punctured Johnson's chest. Blood edged out of the new wound.

The man lay still, his eyes closed, looking for all the world as if he were asleep.

TWENTY-SEVEN

Spur took both Johnson's and McCormick's bodies back to Fargo. On his way he figured what had happened. Johnson's wife and children had been killed by Northern army raiders during the war. Johnson had been haunted by this and it had turned him insane.

Somehow he came to the idea that every "Yankee" with whom he came in contact—at least the men he knew to be Northerners—had been those who'd murdered his family, and he did not hesitate to do what he felt justified in doing. He killed them.

He'd assembled his raiders to aid him in these projects. Spur had no way of knowing how much about Johnson's past the raiders were aware of, and he probably never would know. Johnson was dead and the raiders were disbanded. He'd carried out his orders.

The ride to Fargo took roughly six hours, since he was leading two horses and wasn't in a hurry. By

219

the time he rode past Kelly's Saloon the horses were tired and hungry. He tied all three at a rail opposite hte jail and thought about the two bodies.

To whom should he give them? The sheriff was dead. His deputy? He remembered the brash young man who'd hounded him during his incarceration.

Spur left the horses, ignoring the crowd that gathered around them, and walked into the jail. Herman sat behind the desk.

"Herman, McCormick's dead."

"What?" The man paled.

"He was wounded by Rontrell's men and died a few hours later. Rontrell's dead as well. His real name is Clint Johnson. I have both bodies out front."

"I—I don't understand," Herman said, confused, his face flushing.

"You'd better. You're the sheriff now."

He turned and left the office. One more piece of unfinished business—Johnson had mentioned Francine. His sister, Lila had told him.

He strode down Main Street, turned up Elm and climbed the steps of the house, weariness stabbing through him. He rang the bell and waited. In a moment the door opened and a tense woman of forty, elegantly dressed, stood before him.

"Francine Johnson?"

She was startled to see him. "Yes."

"Could you come with me? I think the sheriff has a few questions for you."

"I don't understand." She smiled, but Spur saw the nervousness behind it.

"Your brother is dead."

She clasped her hands before her. "Dear God."

"I know he was Rontrell. So does the sheriff. And I believe you were involved in his activities. He implicated you before he died."

The woman shook her head and moved to a chair near the front door. She didn't cry. "I knew it. I knew if he pursued this it would lead to his death."

Spur was silent, listening.

"He was so proud in the beginning. When I found out what he was doing he boasted like a boy describing a favorite puppy. I knew he wasn't quite sane. He wasn't a lunatic but he did have his moments." Her chin bobbed. "My God, he's dead. I tried to warm him about you." She glared at him. "You. You're responsible. You killed him."

He nodded.

"I knew it! I warned him! The pigheaded man wouldn't listen. If he had, none of this would have happened. He was so sure of himself, bragging how he'd fooled you completely. I should have killed you myself, that first time I saw you on the street with that Fairley woman. But I didn't. I waited—and now he's dead."

She stood. Spur grasped her wrists, unsure if she'd attempt to resist, but she did not. He led her from the house and down to Main Street, where Herman had had the bodies laid out.

"I've got a prisoner for you," Spur said to Herman. "She was part of their operation."

Herman had lost his confusion. He was subtly different; the responsibility thrust upon him had matured him. He looked at Francine Johnson.

"Really?"

She nodded.

Herman took the woman into the jail. Spur felt someone touch him. He turned and saw Lila standing behind him.

"Spur, what happened?"

"I don't want to talk about it."

Herman walked up a moment later. "McCoy, I've got a helluva lot of questions for you to answer. I want to know every detail."

"As long as I can get to the telegraph office before it closes."

Herman nodded. Spur looked at Lila and smiled weakly. It was over.

After Spur had answered Herman's questions he went to the wire office and sent a message to General Halleck. Rontrell was dead and the raiders disbanded. He also wired the circumstances which had led Clint Johnson to his actions.

That accomplished, he took a long, hot bath at Lila's boarding house. Despite the strain of the last week he felt strangely refreshed, relaxed and yet full of energy.

He met Lila at Kelly's as he went in for a drink.

"Hello, Spur," she said.

"Hi." They went to the bar and ordered their drinks, then took them to a table.

"What'll you do now?" she asked. "You staying in town?"

"I won't know for a day or two."

"I see. You still won't talk about it?" she asked calmly.

"I can't."

"That's all right. As long as you did what you came here to do." She sipped her beer. "I thought you might like to know. Some men just rode back from the place where you shot the raiders. They said they found Mayor Evans among the dead."

"I see. You'll be electing a new mayor, then." He glanced at her and saw her eyes turn shiny. "Lila, I'm sorry. For everything."

She smiled and sniffled. "Everything?"

"I mean the kidnapping and the fire—I didn't intend you to get involved in that."

"Forget it, Spur. I survived and so did you. That's what we are, Spur—survivors." She sighed. "By the way, Julie took a train today to Denver to check on her insurance. If everything works out she won't be back. She's staying there."

Spur nodded. "So she's a survivor too?"

Lila smiled. "Yes." She lifted her glass. "To survivors."

Spur touched his glass to hers, stared at her lovely face, then downed the whiskey, washing away the bitter memories of the last week, sharpening the sweet ones.

AN ADULT WESTERN ADVENTURE

#8 THE ROBERT E. MILLS

KANSAN

SHOOTOUT AT THE GOLDEN SLIPPER

His was a world of revenge and desire, where the trails and the women were scorching hot!

LEISURE
1044
$2.25

The Kansan lay paralyzed as his arch enemy plucked his beautiful blonde girlfriend from his side — the woman he had traveled across the country twice to rescue.

Despite his injuries, the Kansan must again take up the chase over the searing plains where women are fiery and justice is scarce.

CATEGORY:
Adult Western

PRICE: $2.25
0-8439-1044-5